PRAISE

Winner of the
Nevada Writers Hall of Fame Silver Pen Award

"Throughout the volume's eight tenuously linked tales, lives and fortune are lost, and the city of Reno emerges as a locus of shattered souls. Maynard's debut collection bursts with idiosyncratic characters...packs a strong emotional punch...is strangely entertaining."

—*PUBLISHERS WEEKLY*

"In *Grind*, Maynard reveals a world the Nevada tourism board would rather you didn't see...A debut collection of stories that perfectly captures the seediness, desperation and sense of loss permeating the hot desert world of Reno."

—*SHELF AWARENESS*

"Mark Maynard's Reno is so sleazily appealing, so filled with convict cowboys, wild horses, racing pilots, truckers, snow bums, eco-terrorists, tattoo conventions, pawnshops and jackpots that you emerge from reading *Grind* dazed by this author's empathy for neglected quarters of humanity. You feel gritty all over—and more alive."

—CAROLYN COOKE,
author of *DAUGHTERS OF THE REVOLUTION*

"The characters in these stories are as beautiful and broken as the desert itself. Mark Maynard explores the stony truths of lost lives with an unflinching eye for detail, an insider's sense of the place and its people, and an honest compassion. The heartbreaks here are real, as are the moments of uncommon grace and hard-won redemption."

—KIM BARNES,
author of *IN THE KINGDOM OF MEN*

"Mark Maynard's *Grind* is chock full of men and women who are desperate with want and full of spirit. Pawnbrokers. Truckers. Casino shills. Prison inmates. They're all here, and they're all gloriously alive. This is prime American fiction-- tough, generous, and open-eyed."

—ALYSON HAGY,
author of *BOLETO*

"It includes stories about casinos, wild horses, prostitutes, air races, long-haul truck drivers—you know, the stuff that makes Northern Nevada great. *Grind* is exactly what I like in a locally based book. Lots of stories about the gritty realism in and around Reno. Plenty of those characters who make a visit to the environs of Reno both an exciting potential and an illicit affair…This is a Northern Nevada book."

—D. BRIAN BURGHART,
RENO NEWS & REVIEW

GRIND

Stories by

Mark Maynard

GRIND

Stories by

Mark Maynard

TORREY HOUSE PRESS

SALT LAKE CITY • TORREY

First Torrey House Press Edition, December 2012
Copyright © 2012 by Mark Maynard

Published by Torrey House Press, LLC
Salt Lake City, Utah
torreyhouse.org

International Standard Book Number: 978-1-937226-03-9
Library of Congress Control Number: 2012938796

Cover photographs by Guy Tal, Guy Tal Photography,
www.guytal.com
Author photo by Tom Seawell
Cover by Jeff Fuller, Crescent Moon Communications

For Reno, and its resilient people.

CONTENTS

PROLOGUE

*G*rind.
This town will wear you down from the outside until all that remains is dust. Reno has always been a place where rough men and women have been able to find work in good times and trouble has been able to find them in bad ones.

In the turbulent wake of pilgrims, argonauts and buckaroos rolled the grifters, tradesmen, thugs, and junkies. The divorce trade and gambling (referred to locally as the more sporting term, "gaming") rolled through like the Truckee River.

Everything and everyone here was once something or someone else. City Hall sits on the edge of the river in a black glass high-rise that was once the hotel portion of one of the original casinos after it had been a bank. Many of the casinos themselves have been shuttered or are being converted to condos, the first few conversion projects of which have also been boarded up, awaiting their next transformation.

Bisecting town is Virginia Street, the old north-south thoroughfare that was replaced years ago by an elevated freeway. The heart of town can still be found on Virginia Street, between First and Fourth, not far from Myron Lake's original bridge. There, staring at one another across the avenue, sit the Mother Lode Hotel and Casino and the Taj Mahal pawnshop, each a major part of the machine that recycles money and the people who chase it around town. These businesses cater to everyone from the casual tourist to the longtime local, destitute

1

and looking to play his last dollar or pawn his last power tool or family heirloom. The owners of these two establishments would tell you they are providing a unique and necessary service to their community. And if they didn't do it, somebody else would.

The finest cities, like the most elegant ships, are always anthropomorphized into female form. Paris is known for *her* romantic lights, New York for *her* moxie and bustle. But Reno is decidedly male. And what with his smoking, constant drinking, lack of sleep and poor diet, he is not aging gracefully. And then there is the "gaming," a linguistic trick sprung on the lifeblood tourists to make giving one's money up in games of "chance" romanticized into a classy occupation—a dying industry that, just like any insufferable, addicted gambler, this city is not quite able to give up, even for *his* best interests.

Ancient casinos still cater to a chain-smoking, tight-fisted, nickel-slot-playing crowd. These handle-pull undertakers make you work for every filthy nickel. In these old gaming halls, the carpets are worn and stained. The drink glasses are opaque with a carnival glass haze that can't be washed out— etched ghosts of eons of lipstick and cigarette smoke coat them inside and out.

Reno takes all comers—which is a good thing, because it is often a final destination for those on a downward spiral. As Woody Guthrie, Johnny Cash, Tom Waits, and the Grateful Dead knew, it was the perfect city for song lyrics—four letters and two syllables encompassing a world of desolation and destitution: *Re-no.*

It is not a town devoid of culture. Home to two of the largest tattoo conventions in the nation (not only are there rows of ink parlors downtown and in the suburbs, there is also a parlor in the shopping mall, wedged between Macy's and a beauty salon). For those not enamored of the art of body illustration, the annual Arttown Festival hosts international chamber orchestras and the likes of Yo-Yo Ma and Mikhail Baryshnikov in front of sold out houses of Renoites. The mansions of Myron Lake and his contemporaries have been turned into theaters, art centers and independent bookstores, and the garages, workshops and warehouses are often filled year-round with designers, builders and mad scientists hard at work on their otherworldly vehicles and domiciles for the Burning Man festival held north of town in the Black Rock Desert. Whenever two opposite forces come together, there is friction.

Reno, Nevada, is a border town in every sense. *La Frontera Nueva*. The New Frontier. Set in a low spot at the eastern root of the Sierra, the city stays true to its genesis, when Myron Lake's toll crossing established its very existence over 160 years ago. The hyped-up, oxymoronic "Biggest Little City" tag is a misnomer for a sprawling cluster of stucco suburbs set on dried up cattle ranches. Reno is, and always will be, a town.

It straddles the ideals of California to the west and the independent mountain states that ring the Great Basin Desert to the east. It is a place where trucks stop on the lonely Interstate 80 that winds over the infamous Donner Pass on the western way to Sacramento and crosses endless desert east of town, finally pushing its way over the Great Plains and on to Ocean City, Maryland. It gets a small share of the annual snowfall that blankets the Sierra, yet spends most of the time parched, sitting on the edge of the desert while the trickling Truckee River feeds its ever growing thirst.

Every girl who dances in the bars and clubs knows that the right amount of friction can squeeze money from a man's pocket. Once the first single has been pried forth, the rest flows unabated: fives, tens, twenties. Depending on how long and hard one wants to work, the money will follow. One more way this town wears people down. Life here can rough anyone and anything up, raising burrs that become metal shavings in a crankcase, finally causing the engine to seize.

It's always been a good town for a bender. A second home for miscreants, petty thieves, and whores who come for the weekend to see whose pockets they can get into when hordes of plump Americans pack the downtown streets to gawk at cars, cowboys, racing airplanes, or dentists and chiropractors living out biker fantasies. It's a dream locale for ski bums who can't find couch space in any of the few, rapidly disappearing, dilapidated ski condos at Lake Tahoe and must settle for dingy apartments near their dishwashing and floor mopping jobs, minutes away from the fresh powder and steep slopes they live for.

Cutting through the glittering night-heart of town rolls the massive blacktop ribbon of Interstate 80—Reno is a permanent station on the always moving bi-coastal commerce line whose 18-wheel diesel locomotives cannot be confined to iron rails.

But underneath the lawless six-gun mythos is a town where the men and women live with a unique kind of hope. Like the scent of rain on sagebrush, there is always the promise that something might bloom there on the desert floor. As if Prosperity himself might be one of the strangers walking through town and across the river on his way somewhere else. This town knows it is not Las Vegas, and takes great pride in that fact. The folks who live here know that a better day is coming and it may as well be tomorrow.

And so, into the grind a collection of strangers, part of the always moving and interconnected group of people who call Reno home, if only for a little while.

JACKPOT

Timothy Kelleher was headed straight for the buffet when someone called his name. He was hoping that Bobby, the coffee shop manager, was working today, and that if he paid his five bucks he would be allowed to take the table in the corner and eat his meal in peace. He'd been saving the money he'd panhandled all week and showered at the shelter last night, slipping into the cleanest clothes he owned.

He hated walking through the casinos. The lights, the noise, the crowd all set him on edge. Weird things happened to people in here. There was treachery and danger lurking in the wide open. He bolted across the casino floor. The less time spent in the chaos, the better. He found the first sign—"Buffet"—and kept his eyes locked on it until he found the next one along his way.

"Tim. Tim. TIM!"

He froze. The voice came from a bank of slot machines. He turned to see who could possibly know his name in here. A blinking row of machines stared back at him. They laughed, mumbling things he could not quite hear. He wanted to run, either to the buffet or out the door—but he did not have a direct shot at either one.

"Tim. Sit down."

The old-style reel machine on the end stared at him with three glowing eyes. The pupil of the first was a large 7, the middle one was a polar bear, and the last one said "ICE." The

7 winked at him, and the machine's one good arm beckoned him over with its useless little knob hand.

Terrified, Tim walked over to the slots and sat on the vinyl swivel stool in front of the machine. He looked in its middle eye, his shoulders hunched, and awaited instructions.

"Good," said the machine. "Now feed me, you dirty bum."

Tim stared blankly.

"Your money. The ten dollars in your coat pocket. Feed it to me."

That's my money, he thought. *I stood outside all day yesterday to get enough for the coffee shop. Fuck you. I should rip your goddamn arm off.* The machine stared back. Cold. Unblinking. Tim knew better than to argue. He reached for the small square of folded bills—his breakfast money. Pancakes and coffee with a side of sausage. Tim fed the money into the machine's tight-lipped mouth; the lower part had a picture of a dollar on it, showing which way the machine liked to eat its bills.

Joe Cotter's stomach woke him eleven minutes before his alarm. An intense cramp and loud gurgle insisted he needed to run for the bathroom. It took his sleep-addled brain a minute to register this fact, and he barely made it the required ten feet in time.

When he was done, he assessed the situation. What had he eaten for dinner last night? Was anybody at work sick? He knew a shower would make him feel better and help him decide if this were a one-time thing, or if he needed to call in sick.

He sat on the molded plastic floor of his shower and lowered his head, exposing the back of his neck to the jets of water from above. The crackling static of the hot rain pelted the leather of his ears and back of his skull. The heat cascaded down his face and dripped off his nose into the drain. His shivering body ached. He decided he would call in to the 24-hour Casino Monitoring Desk at High Desert Gaming as soon as he got warmed from the shower and had a cup of hot tea. He would spend the day in bed, a rare occurrence.

Ten minutes into his shower, his pager chirped on the vanity counter.

He had no choice now. He was going to work, intestinal distress or not. He stepped from the shower and toweled off. He ambled to the kitchen and picked up his cordless phone, punching in the secure number he knew was on his pager.

"Casino Monitoring, this is Greg speaking."

"Greg, Joe Cotter. The bells and whistles went off, what have we got?"

"Morning, Joe. Better get down here now. Twelve point two million on the SuperJackpot!"

"Jesus! Another sweet little blue-haired millionaire?"

"No. This one's a guy. Fifties. Sounds like he's homeless or something. This one's going to be interesting."

Terrific.

"Thanks, Greg, I'll be by in fifteen minutes to pick up the kit."

Greg explained that the casino staff had already cordoned off the machine and was no doubt plying the winner with tons of free drinks. Joe thanked him again and hung up.

First the bowels, then the pager. Now he got to spend the rest of the morning trying to get ID off a bum whom the cocktail waitresses would probably have bombed out of his mind by the time he got there.

It took Lucy Diaz two minutes and seven seconds to make her way from her tech booth to the flashing lights and screaming buzzers in the SuperJackpot section of the dollar slot corral. She could've navigated the casino floor in utter darkness, but even she was unable to walk a straight line across the festively carpeted room the size of four football fields. She was not susceptible to the traps built by the casino's designers. Lucy knew that, in Reno, the shortest distance between here and there was most definitely not a straight line. She walked around the banks of slot machines and down, across rows of gaming tables intercepting anyone walking toward the restrooms, the buffet, the hotel elevators, and, most importantly, the exit.

She waited, out of view, until Ray and Tony from security met her. Together, the three of them rounded the corner and saw the terrified man in front of the "Ice Cold Cash" three-reel slot, a trio of sunglasses-wearing penguins standing in front of an igloo silk-screened on its glass panel.

Lucy approached the man as Ray and Tony herded the gathering crowd back from the machine, arms outstretched and hands hip-high, gesturing, "Move back, move back please, folks."

"Good morning, sir. My name is Lucy Diaz, and I am a slot technician for High Desert Gaming. If you will remain here until our Jackpot Response Team arrives, we will begin the process of verifying your win. Meanwhile, I'm going to open the machine up and quiet this thing down. Excuse me."

Lucy took a knee at the front of the machine and stuck a key into a lock hidden on the lower panel concealing the cashbox. She flipped a switch just inside the metal door, silencing the bells and extinguishing the flashing lights. She stood, turning to face the man still sitting stiffly in the chair. His hair was tangled and damp. A thick beard rose from the neck of his flannel shirt and stopped just below his watery, vacant eyes. His lips were moving; he was speaking, but not to her. His down vest shed feathers through a small hole. His blue jeans sprouted light cotton threads from holes in the knees and were stained with grease and patches of dried human moisture.

Timothy Kelleher glanced at the attractive woman standing in front of him, then looked away.

"Now you've done it! You broke Nanook." A yellow caution light like the one atop the street sweepers that roused him from alleyways in the early morning hours accused him. "You're in trouble, Tim. Don't you try to hide. You stay right there and take what's coming to you."

His body was still in the standing tuck he used to make himself invisible. His hands covered his crotch. His shoulders stooped and he kept his head down, staring at the garish confetti and hot air balloon pattern on the carpet. If he looked long enough, the balloons rose from the floor and floated gracefully a few inches above it while the confetti streamers writhed and sparkled. The woman. Lucy, he thought she said. Lucy in a sky of balloons and confetti. She told him to stay, so stay he would. Tim folded his arms across his chest and clutched his shoulders, rocking in his seat. This made him feel a little better.

Joe Cotter's head was pounding by the time he pulled through the security gate at High Desert Gaming. Joe parked beneath the still lit "HDG" letters, visible halfway across the valley. It was dark still in the early morning shadow of the building, and he buzzed himself through the security doors, placing his outstretched fingers on the biometric pad, gaining entry into the secure Jackpot Monitoring Center.

The onsite team had already mobilized and had his kit ready. He had made dozens of large payouts, but the cashier's check for "twelve million two hundred thousand dollars and no/100s" looked ridiculous. Somehow, the giant cardboard check covering an entire folding tabletop just inside the doorway looked better suited to such a sum. Sam Cohen, Joe's partner on the Jackpot Verification Team, was already dressed in his navy blazer with the HDG logo on the breast and was helping pack up the locking briefcase they would take with them to the Mother Lode.

"You're late, Joe."

"Flu. Shouldn't even be here."

"Nice. Don't get me sick." Cohen finished packing up the case and locked one latch with his key. He made an exaggerated step away from Joe and placed the forearm of his blazer across his nose and mouth like a third world doctor moving amongst cots in a makeshift cholera ward. Sam watched Joe lock the other latch on the case as he signed them out in the logbook, and they left through a side door, which led them directly to an HDG van parked outside. Sam unlocked and opened the back doors, and Joe placed the case inside the security cage. Sam offered to drive, telling Joe he didn't want to die in a flu-induced wreck.

"I hear that our winner is a riverfront bum." Sam laughed. "Want to just stay in the van?"

Joe smiled. "Yeah, I'll just curl up in the back and sleep—you won't mind, will you?"

"I pretty much do this job by myself anyway."

Sam pulled the van out of the security gates and down the small road behind the complex. Two minutes later he merged with traffic on US 395 North and sped toward downtown.

"Pull off at the next exit!" Joe's voice hit a falsetto note of urgency.

"What? We're going to the Mother Lode. We need to get off at—"

"I know where we need to go, but I'm not going to make it that far. Pull off!"

"Are you kidding me? Where the hell am I going to stop for you?"

"I don't care, just get off the damn road and pull over!"

Another wave of cramps had hit Joe.

"Goddammit, Cotter. You're going to get us both fired."

Sam exited the freeway and turned right at the bottom of the off-ramp. There was a small strip mall surrounded by hundreds of homes that had swallowed up the meadows and wetlands thriving there not ten years earlier. Everything in the mall was still closed at this hour.

"Shit! Keep going." Joe's voice stretched thin, and his breath leaked out between pursed lips.

"You want me to drive through the subdivision, or get back on the freeway?" Sam did not feel it was his duty to come up with a plan. He was just the driver.

"I gotta go now! Go into the neighborhood!"

Sam drove down the parkway and turned into the first subdivision on their right—MacDonald Ranch. Sam cruised down cul de sacs and quiet streets named after flowers that did not grow anywhere in Northern Nevada. He parked on the street in front of a house whose front windows were glowing with light.

Joe pleaded with Sam to come to the door with him. Sam told Joe he was on his own and reminded him the casino would be calling HDG to see where they were soon. He relented when he watched his partner hobbling up the front walk, half-doubled by cramps. Sam overtook Joe before he reached the doorstep.

"What are you gonna tell 'em? We're the city toilet inspectors?"

"I need to get to a bathroom. Now." Joe knew he was a pitiful sight, doubled over on the covered, stucco-front porch.

"Jesus Christ, Cotter. You are one helpless son of a bitch."

Joe rang the doorbell. It took at least two minutes before an older woman came to the front window and peered at them. Joe tried to appear friendly, waving at the eyes peering at him through a slit in the vertical blinds. They heard a deadbolt unlatch, and the front door opened a crack.

"May I help you, gentlemen? It's awfully early—"

"Sorry to bother you, ma'am. We saw the lights were on, so..." Joe's guts twisted.

Sam stood quietly behind Joe. He was obviously going to be no help.

"We're from HDG and we're on our way to a call, and there's a problem with our van. Do you think we could possibly borrow your telephone?"

"Why don't you just call them on your cellular phone, or a radio or something?" she asked. Suspicion was the only protector of little old women who lived alone.

"Uh, we're in a dead zone here. No reception. And I was also wondering if I might use your bathroom."

"What do you do for HDG?" Joe had a feeling they were not going to get in. He was minutes from soiling himself on the woman's front porch.

Sam remained silent.

"We verify and award jackpots, ma'am. We're actually on our way to verify a jackpot right now, so we're kind of pressed for time. If I could just use your..."

"Let me see your business cards."

Joe clutched at the breast pocket of his blazer, where he sometimes stashed a small stack of cards. It was empty.

Lucy Diaz remained at the slot machine as required. There were no obvious signs that it had been tampered with, but she still had to run several diagnostic tests, which could take thirty minutes or more. She sensed that the winner, still mumbling on the stool behind her, was not doing well. She called to the two security guards, and Ray turned to look at her. She gestured him over to the machine.

12

"Can we move our guy somewhere off the casino floor? Maybe get him somewhere quiet, give him a cup of coffee and hang out with him until the jackpot team gets here? I'm afraid he's sort of freakin' out with this crowd gathering."

Ray rolled his eyes at Lucy and spoke into his radio. A garbled voice punched through the air from the speaker and he nodded to Lucy.

"Sir." Lucy touched the man's shoulder and felt him flinch, his muscles tense. "Sir, these nice men would like to take you somewhere much quieter and off the casino floor." Tim did not respond.

"Sir, if you would just go with them, these nice gentlemen are going to take you to a nice quiet office until the jackpot people come."

Finally, Tim spoke. "No!"

"Sir?"

"I'm not going with them! I didn't do anything wrong!" Tim pushed his forearm to his forehead and wrapped his other arm around his gut, trying to protect his soft, vulnerable places. "Please just let me go. I won't tell anybody what happened, I swear!"

"My name is Lucy. This is Ray, and his partner is Tony. We are all here to help you. We thought you might like to get out of this noise and get a cup of coffee."

"Do you have food?"

"Anything you would like. Just tell us, and we'll order it from the coffee shop right away."

"Pancakes," Tim said. He said it eleven times. After two minutes of rhythmic rocking and chanting, Tim stopped. Lucy set her hand on his forearm, guiding him to his feet.

The slots and tables yelled at him as he walked past. Their lights flashed in accusation. He was forced to weave among the banks of the glowing machines, avoiding their outstretched handles and their video screens that blinked out secret messages in runes and symbols. "You killed Big Nanook!" they called. "Hey Tim, what'd you do to poor Nanook? What'd you feed him, anyway? One of your dirty street bills?"

Ray and Tony didn't seem to notice the machines laughing and screaming Tim's name as they walked through the blinking neon labyrinth. Tim stepped on the back of Tony's black loafer while trying to avoid a colorful eel rocking back and forth in the calm sea of carpet, which was coated in an oilslick of iridescent colors.

"Sorry," Tim mumbled.

"Watch where you're walking, you trash-eater!" The high-pitched voice came from beneath the vinyl cover of a dormant blackjack table. The small engraved plastic sign on top read, "Mother Lode Casino/Split Any Pair/Dealer Must Hit On Soft 17/Tim Is An Eskimo Killer."

"Where are you going, Timmy?" A machine mocked him as he walked past.

"Pancakes."

"How much did you win, Tim?"

"Pancakes."

Tim pushed himself between Ray and Tony, sensing they would not lead him into the pack of predatory gaming devices. The three men reached the bottom of an escalator, and Tony gestured for Tim to follow Ray on board so that he had one security guard in front and one behind him. It was the safest he'd felt all morning.

"Pancakes." He smiled back at Tony.

"That's right," Tony said, stifling a laugh. "All the pancakes you want, buddy."

Joe Cotter ran through the hallway of Janice Gridley's suburban Spanish-style home and headed straight for the small half bath featured in her "Sage Ridge" floor plan layout. While Joe was occupied, Janice grilled Sam.

"Don't you need to make a call? Phone's in the kitchen."

"Oh. Thank you, ma'am. Joe makes the calls, I just drive."

"I don't believe that for a second. Nice young man like you. So what do you two do, exactly?"

"We verify jackpots, ma'am." Sam was pissed. Cotter has the shits, so he has to get interviewed by decrepit old women? At least they could have found some hot chick's door to knock on at six-thirty in the morning. Maybe then she'd just be getting dressed or stepping out of the shower or something. Joe owed Sam, and he owed him big. If they didn't get rolling soon, they could get reassigned to a new territory. That was what happened when you were no longer a top team. You decomposed in the cow counties, chasing thousand-dollar jackpots in truck stops and mini marts. Elko. Hawthorne. West Wendover.

Mrs. Gridley asked Sam about the biggest jackpot he'd ever verified. Sam was not about to volunteer that locked in the briefcase in the back of the van was a check for twelve million dollars and change. They were never supposed to leave that briefcase unattended. *Cotter's asshole is going to cost me my job,* he thought as the old woman droned on about her gambling exploits. Sam kept thinking about the hot chick that hadn't let them in. She was tall and blonde and came to the door in her bra and panties. These weren't your everyday bra and panties, either. They were the ones in the display window at the Chocolate Walrus on Old Virginia Street, sheer and white lace through which you could see the blonde's…

"Do you think we should check on your friend?" The old woman seemed concerned. Sam couldn't tell if it was for Joe or for her guest bathroom.

Just then, Joe emerged from the bathroom. His face was pale and haggard. His hair was soaked in sweat.

"Let's go, Cotter. We're already ten minutes overdue."

Jesus. Joe knew that they were taking too long for a top team. *Shoulda called in sick.*

"Right." Joe turned to face their hostess. "Thank you, ma'am."

"Didn't you want to use the phone?"

"Uh, it turns out that I don't need to call after all. Thanks anyway." Joe said this with his back turned to her as he made for the door and the van outside.

Sam passed Joe about halfway across the grass and had the van unlocked by the time Joe reached the passenger door. Sam hefted his bulk into the driver's seat and put the key in the ignition.

"No more stops, Cotter. If you've gotta go again, you wait until we get there, or you hold it. Understand me?" As he spoke, he turned the key. The starter engaged, but the motor would not turn over.

"Ease off the gas. You're going to flood it!" Joe knew nothing about cars, but it made him feel a little better to tell Sam what to do. It helped reassure him that this was all somehow Sam's fault. Sam tried to start the van seven more times, grinding the teeth of the starter.

"Should we call it in?" Joe offered.

"And tell them what, that our van is broken down in front of some old lady's house in MacDonald Ranch?"

Sam was right. It was strictly forbidden for any Jackpot Verification Team to do anything or go anywhere other than straight to the assigned location. This was a security protocol to help protect not only the millions of dollars the team carried with them, but also to protect the team itself. All of the vans had GPS tracking devices installed in them, but the one Sam and Joe drove had a wiring problem and hadn't ever worked properly. Their van couldn't be tracked on the monitors back at HDG headquarters, which suited both men.

Joe shifted in his seat. Sam was still. They looked out the windshield at the cluster of neighboring houses, each built in one of four exterior styles and painted slightly different shades of beige.

Sam sighed and placed his forehead on the crown of the steering wheel, then turned to face Joe, warning him that if the van didn't start in three minutes he was calling in.

"Are you insane? What are you going to tell them?"

"That we broke down and that they should ready another team to come and pick up the briefcase."

"And where are you going to tell them we are?"

"What do you expect me to do? You've screwed us both! They're going to be wondering why we haven't arrived yet."

Joe tried to explain why they couldn't just send another team. They don't just cut twelve-million-dollar checks twice in a day. He asked his partner to stay off the radio for five more minutes and climbed out the passenger door.

Joe made his way back to Janice Gridley's front porch. He didn't need to ring the bell—she had been watching them from her window. She opened the door and asked, "What is it now, Joe?"

"Mrs. Gridley! Hello again. You know what? I completely forgot to use your phone. Do you think I—"

"You poor boy. Stay right there and let me make you some soup." The old woman had her hand to his forehead. She turned, leaving him on the porch, and crossed a small open living room, stepping behind a counter separating her entryway from the kitchen.

"It's still breakfast, but I think I have some chicken noodle in here somewhere…"

Joe saw a cordless phone on the countertop behind her, its voicemail light blinking like an orange strobe.

"I'm sorry, Mrs. Gridley. You're right. I'm not feeling all that well. But Sam and I are in a hurry. If I could just come in and use your phone."

"I suppose your friend might want a bowl, too." She'd begun digging in a small pantry closet.

Joe felt like kicking the little resin angel statue on her porch in frustration. He also felt like stepping over the threshold and into the kitchen, leaning over to cry on her grandmotherly shoulder.

One doesn't get on the Jackpot Response Team without being able to maintain a cool detachment and knowing how to read the emotions and desires of others. As soon as he'd seen Mrs. Gridley, he'd detected in her a deep-seated desire to be important in someone's life. This could easily overcome her distrust of outsiders.

"Mrs. Gridley. This is a matter of extreme importance to my partner and myself. It is also a matter of extreme importance to my company, to which I am very loyal. We have a bit of an emergency situation here, and should you decide to assist us in this very delicate and pressing matter, you would not only have my gratitude but that of my company."

My God, he thought, *what bullshit.*

"Well…" her disembodied voice trailed out from behind her louvered pantry door. "You boys did show up at my house, unannounced, very early this morning." She continued rummaging through the nearly empty shelves, and Joe realized she was embarrassed—she had nothing to offer him. He began formulating an apology for bothering her at such an early hour. Sam's voice from behind him was a surprise.

"As my partner here was probably telling you, we have a very tight deadline, and we need to be leaving immediately. Trouble is, our van won't go anywhere, and if we can't get someone out here soon, then all your kindness and assistance to HDG's top-rated Jackpot Response Team has been in vain."

Joe turned around to see Sam grinning maniacally, holding various items of promotional swag taken from the floor of their van. *Jesus Christ*, thought Joe, *he's the ultimate door-to-door salesman.*

"As a token of our appreciation, ma'am," Sam continued, "we'd like to give you a lifetime membership in the HDG Golden Circle Club, which includes this limited edition sweatshirt—a very rare and very hot commodity."

Sam displayed a Golden Circle sweatshirt, holding it in front of him by the shoulders. Across the front was the HDG logo encircled by a gaudy gold ring. The Golden Circle was a sales award given at the annual corporate banquet to the top salesperson in each region. Joe had no idea how it had ended up on the floor of their van.

Mrs. Gridley emerged from the pantry, and her large eyes, clouded by age and sleep, focused on the HDG junk that Sam was showing off like some game show model. She approached the two men in her doorway, squinting to get a better look at the sweatshirt.

Sam continued. "Ma'am. We are very sorry that we bothered you this morning. Obviously, we have strayed from protocol. Unfortunately, there is another sweet woman very much like yourself that is about to have her life changed when we show up with a check and verify her jackpot. Now, you have to understand that we don't just show up with paperwork and a check. No, you see, Joe and I are trained to help people deal with the psychological aspects of winning such a large sum of money..."

Joe wanted to nominate Sam for the Golden Circle Award right there on the spot. The man could bullshit.

"Now, Mrs. Gridley," Sam was on a roll, "if you could continue to assist us in delivering our special cargo to that woman downtown, we would be very grateful."

Joe felt more rumbling in his stomach. He needed to use the phone, and then the bathroom again, and they needed a tow truck, a ride, and a top notch excuse if they wanted to keep their jobs.

Lucy finished checking the main processor and re-verifying everything on the machine. The win was legitimate. The obviously down-on-his-luck guy up in the security office was now a multimillionaire. She grabbed her toolkit and headed upstairs to inform the assembling mass of casino executives, security guards, and gawkers that the win was indeed legitimate, at least from the machine's point of view. The security tapes had most likely already been viewed to see if Timothy Kelleher was actually the one sitting at the machine when it hit.

She felt flush. It was her job to keep the programmed machines running perfectly, not to deal with the winners. She wished the Jackpot Response Team would arrive. She was tense and finding it hard to catch a full breath. Twelve million dollars was such an unfathomable amount, and her connection with this win gave her a weird feeling in the pit of her stomach, like she had just witnessed a horrible car accident, had extracted the victims from the smoking wreck, and was waiting for the paramedics to arrive. Strange that someone else's good fortune should make her so…apprehensive. But she kept wondering, in the back of her mind, if it was good fortune after all. She was afraid that Mr. Kelleher had no idea what he was in for.

Tim sat in a small conference room in the hotel's security office, devouring his second stack of pancakes. They had been slathered in three tiny paper cups of whipped butter and drenched in maple syrup. As he ate, the outer office began to fill up with people. They were wearing suits and dresses, and they were all gawking at him through the conference room windows. They were talking in hushed tones, but he knew it was about him. Word had probably gotten around that he'd killed Nanook—though he still didn't know how. It was strange, being noticed by so many people. Many of them had, at one time or another, passed right by him on the streets outside. Ray and Tony sat across the table.

"How do you like your pancakes, man?" Ray asked him.

Tim grunted and kept eating.

"Want some more food, Mr. Kelleher?" Tony asked.

Tim shook his head and mouthed a fork overloaded with dripping flapjacks. A balding man in a designer suit caught Tony's attention through the conference room window and motioned him into the outer office.

"Excuse me if I step out for a moment, Mr. Kelleher. Enjoy your breakfast and let Ray here know if we can get you anything." Tony slipped out of the conference room and into the outer office, where he was greeted by John Ramos, General Manager of the Mother Lode Hotel and Casino. The GM wanted to know how the winner was holding up.

"Right now he's just enjoying a complementary pancake breakfast."

"I can see that. I just finished viewing the tapes and meeting with the HDG technician and it appears on our end that this is a valid jackpot."

"Wow. Twelve million. Gonna change this dude's life a whole lot, I'll tell you that. Is the jackpot team here yet?"

"No. I have no idea what's holding them up. If they're not here in another ten minutes I'm going to call the supervisor and see what's going on."

"Alright. I think we can keep this guy busy for that long. Let me know when they get here so we can prep him for the show."

When anyone hit a jackpot worth over a thousand dollars at the Mother Lode, the promotional machine kicked into high gear. Every winner got his or her picture taken with John Ramos, a giant cardboard check, and at least two or three of the showgirls from "Eureka! An Erotic Extravaganza," which played in the Comstock showroom every night. These portraits were posted on the Wall of Winners in the hotel lobby, along with a brass plaque engraved with the winner's name and hometown. Ramos was already here and ready, and two of the showgirls, Rita and Elizabeth, were on their way in to get costumed and made up. The star of this circus, Timothy Kelleher, sat in the conference room filling a ceramic cup from a large carafe of piping hot coffee with one hand while lapping butter and syrup from the filthy fingers of the other.

Sam called Truckee Meadows Towing and requested a large flatbed with a reliable driver.

The two members of the Jackpot Response Team had promised Mrs. Gridley a genuine, pull-handle, three-reel nickel machine for her family room. These were occasionally decommissioned and offered to employees and their families for a couple hundred bucks. The promise of her own conversation piece slot machine and the lifetime membership in the Golden Circle Club seemed to gain the old woman's trust. She not only let Sam use the telephone, but also offered Joe her master bathroom. He'd rummaged under her sink and through her medicine cabinets until he found an expired box of over-the-counter anti-diarrheal pills, popping three into his mouth.

The tow truck showed up seven minutes later, and Sam and Joe said their farewells to Mrs. Gridley, setting up a tentative date to deliver her slot machine. Sam supervised as the driver hoisted the van onto the bed of the truck. The three men climbed into the cab and headed downtown.

The driver took them into the narrow alley behind the Mother Lode and the Safari Club Cabaret and double-parked the tow truck near a loading dock. Sam and Joe unlocked the back of the van and removed the Jackpot Verification Kit, hustling inside the unmarked entrance leading past Human Resources and to the service elevator. Joe's stomach, feeling better for the first time all day, knotted up again as he imagined what might await them when the elevator doors parted.

Joe and Sam were ushered into the conference room where Tim was hard at work on his third stack of pancakes. Sam began his monologue. "Mr. Kelleher, on behalf of HDG and the Mother Lode Casino, I would like to personally congratulate you on winning what amounts to the second-largest jackpot ever awarded by our company. Before I can give you this check, we need you to fill out some verification…and of course some tax paperwork, and then we can go downstairs and get your picture taken."

"My picture taken?"

"Yes, Mr. Kelleher. Here's one of the forms we'll have you sign." Sam pulled a paper from the center of the sheaf. "It's a release allowing HDG and the Mother Lode to use your name and image for marketing and promotional purposes."

"You mean they're going to put my picture up?" Tim let his fork drop, clanging, onto his plate. He didn't want people taking his picture and using his name. He lived invisibly next to the Truckee River, and now his picture was going up in one of the city's busiest buildings?

Sam pulled the top form from the stack and handed it across the table to Tim, who looked down at it blankly and then up at Joe. Joe ignored the stabbing cramp just below the waistline of his grey pleated trousers and grabbed the pen Sam had placed on top of the form. "Mr. Kelleher, I'm going to ask you a few questions, and we'll make this go as quickly as possible."

Twenty minutes later, Sam and Joe were conferring with John Ramos about how to handle the situation. It was clear that Timothy Kelleher did not exist, at least not to the extent that anyone could hand over a twelve-million-dollar check to him. He had no known Social Security number. He had no bank account and no physical address. But he had legitimately won the jackpot, and it was only a matter of time before the story broke about the homeless winner. There was no way they could refuse to award the money, even though they could legally do so.

"Why don't we go downstairs, take the pictures, and then hold the news until we can get verification?" asked Joe.

"And how do you plan on doing that?" Sam asked.

"Well, he did say that he collects welfare checks and stops by a shelter for showers and a hot meal every now and then. I'll go to the welfare office and see what personal information they have on file—they aren't going to cut him checks without a social."

"We can use the shelter's address," added Ramos. "We could turn this into a real feel-good story. 'Homeless man hits the Mother Lode.'"

"Okay," Sam conceded. "Let's do it."

Tim began to shake and sweat. It had been hours since he'd had a drink, and while the pancakes and coffee sloshed pleasantly in his stomach, he was still awaiting the verdict on his supposed Eskimo-killing. It was hot in the building. He was being led back through the casino in the center of a large throng of people who were jostling to see the bum-turned-multimillionaire. The fact that four security guards, two men in matching blazers with a metal briefcase, and two showgirls wearing sequined bodysuits revealing healthy portions of ass and breast were in the entourage encouraged gawkers.

Tim hid as best he could behind the oversized check that Joe Cotter carried as the group wound its way back to the machine that had started all of this. When the public relations director finally composed the ever-important photo, Tim was catatonic. In the photo, he stands glassy-eyed and filthy, staring somewhere above the camera's line of sight, clutching the top of the cardboard check while the two showgirls, one on each arm, beam at him with wide, seductive smiles.

After the camera's flash pulsed, the public relations director rounded up the supporting players to get names and spellings for the press release, which would be held until Tim's identification could be verified and the payment actually made. Sam had offered to speak on the record about verifying the win if Joe would stay with Tim.

"You guys seem to have quite an affinity," Sam said in the same pleasant voice he had used on Janice Gridley's porch. "Besides, I think you've both shit yourselves today."

Sam, Ramos, and the rest of the group were herded together, and the relaxed atmosphere of a cocktail party broke out on the casino floor. Joe and Tim walked away from the crowd and stood near the still-cordoned dollar slots corral. The beeps of machines and the muddled voices of casino patrons blended into a comforting buzz now that the crowd had dispersed.

"Tim?" Joe couldn't hold out any longer. "I need to make a quick break for the men's room. You wanna walk over that way with me?"

"No, thanks. I don't have to go."

"Right." Joe looked for the shortest route to the restrooms. "Why don't you just hang on to this for a minute, and I'll be right back." He handed Tim the oversized check and speed-walked off toward the front desk.

The Mother Lode security camera tapes show a befuddled Timothy Kelleher turning to say something to the slot machine on which he had hit the largest jackpot ever awarded outside of Las Vegas. He looks at the front of the large cardboard check, places it under his right arm, and walks away from the crowd, toward the back exit leading to a sidewalk along the Truckee River. The camera catches a last shot of Tim, heading east along the riverwalk and sauntering downstream. Although the camera angle does not catch his face full on, it appears he is smiling.

A check made out to Timothy Kelleher in the amount of twelve point two million dollars sits in a manila envelope in a vault at HDG headquarters.

SIRENS

The radio crackled in Gus Shipley's fighter pilot helmet as he coaxed the throttle forward and tapped the stick to maintain his place in the formation of aircraft flying east over rocky slopes.

The voice of the race starter, flying in a small jet less than a hundred feet above Shipley and the rest of the formation, buzzed in his ears: "Line up for start, we are a *Go!*"

Shipley pointed the vibrating nose of his plane toward the old air bases visible in the distant desert. The cockpit smelled of rubber and fuel and blue smoke. He was in the middle of a buzzing swarm of massive, outdated war machines that had been stripped, sculpted, redesigned, and reborn as air racers. Just to his left was the glazed red paintjob of *Baron VR,* a Focke-Wulf Fw190, and off his right wingtip flew *Wild Horse,* a black and yellow checkered P-51 Mustang. He held the English-built Hawker *Sea Fury* steady with the stick in his right hand and felt the levers and control rods inside the aircraft's skeleton respond with gentle pressure. He sat in a humming tunnel of engine and airframe vibrations occasionally punctuated by the static in the earpieces of his helmet. A tinted visor and the blurred forward glimpse through the revolutions of his five propeller blades restricted his view of the world. The stagnant air of the closed Plexiglas bubble prevented him from inhaling as deeply as he would have liked—he could hear the dull

27

rhythm of his labored breathing in his own head.

Shipley knew all of the amped-up air jockeys he was flying alongside in this qualifying heat. They lived to zip into flight suits with military-style embroidery and wings of gold thread spread over their hearts, members of some oft-decorated lost squadron bulging with self pride. Most of these guys were wrench-heads or airline pilots who longed to get away from their flying bus driver status and play World War II ace over the seared rock of Stead, Nevada. They were good pilots—some were great pilots—but mostly they had money to burn and loved burning it. These guys had hard-ons for speed and competition.

Shipley was here for a different reason: he *needed* to win. Victory was his job security, the only sure way to stay on as the Mother Lode Casino's only full-time air racing pilot.

The seven-plane formation spread out as it headed down the Chute, an imaginary wedge of airspace above the rocky flanks of the mountain that plunged toward the desert floor toward the course, each pilot aiming for the space between pylons three and four. The pace plane broke into a high, left-hand turn away from the collected racers.

"Gentlemen, you have a race!"

The formation scattered, each flyer looking for the perfect line to enter the course and gain the advantage he hoped to sustain for nine laps of the nine-mile, pear-shaped course. Shipley ended up in the fourth position coming into the first turn.

He banked hard left and passed the first pylon—nothing more than a corrugated metal barrel fixed to the top of a fifty-foot telephone pole. Despite his 460-miles-an-hour airspeed, as he passed the barrel at eye-level he could make out the facial features of the judges and photographers looking up at him as they huddled around the pole in a colorful herd.

Miles Jay lived for the races. He'd been holding court in the party room above his hangar for days, sleeping in the small, well-appointed bedroom tucked behind his office. He awoke every race morning to the sound of throaty radial engines kicking out the first puff of heavy carbon before thrumming to life.

He'd been too young to fight in World War II, but as a boy living in Southern California, he watched as the squadrons of war-bound fighters rolled off of assembly lines and eventually ferried overseas to Europe and the Pacific. The pilots who flew the fierce metal raptors became his heroes. After a lifetime of shrewd business decisions and a willingness to occasionally flex his muscle with competitors, cheats, and troublemakers, he became one of the most successful casino owners in Nevada. He was the last of his kind in Reno, the only proprietor who refused to sell out to a "gaming" corporation. The elder statesmen Bill Harrah and Harvey Gross had been dead for many years. The Mapes had been demolished and paved over. The big players, card counters, cheats, crime bosses, and small-time operators had all left town. The once glowing hotel towers, glass-walled ramparts that stood guarding the casinos hidden in their bowels, had been converted into artist lofts and condominiums. Many of these now sat empty, awaiting the next come-out roll in the never-ending craps game that used Virginia Street as its green felt table. Even City Hall occupied the upper floors of a former hotel casino that had once been a bank and the chamber of commerce.

As soon as he had the means, Miles Jay began collecting vintage aircraft, starting with several T-6 Texans that were used to train Army Air Corps and Navy fighter pilots heading off to war. It took him years before he found the right airplane to start his own racing team.

Several qualified pilots responded to the ad Miles posted

in several flying magazines: *WANTED: Corporate Pilot based in Reno, NV. Competitive salary, great benefits.* It was the odd closing line of the ad—*Limited Travel*—that appealed most to Gus Shipley.

Before Miles hired him, Gus had been a cargo pilot long enough to pick up good routes—his last one was San Francisco to Hong Kong. That was before he and Deborah had divorced, starting the nasty battle over custody of eight-year-old Lindsay. His frequent international travel and random schedule meant that he would never be able to spend enough time with her as a part-time, single parent—until he lucked into his current job.

Gus was the official Aircraft Ambassador for the Mother Lode Casino. Except for a few weeks before the air races, he spent five days a week in the special "hangar" adjacent to the Mother Lode's casino floor, where he wore his flight suit and gave patrons a tour of Miles's airplane collection: five planes, including *One Tough Mother*. Miles and his crew chief, Dean Swenson, had spent three years modifying the Sea Fury—shrinking the cockpit profile, building a custom engine, cooling system, and propeller, hinging the wings so they could be folded up, allowing the plane to be hauled between the airfield and the casino hangar on a custom trailer.

This job enabled Gus to be home every night, yet still paid him to fly. Throughout the year, he test-piloted the plane after each modification made by Dean and his crew, and was the official competition pilot during the races. Miles had been proud to have one of the few local planes that flew every year, but after a few seasons, he put a lot of pressure on Gus and Dean to start bringing him victories.

Twenty minutes after Gus clambered out of the tiny cockpit, he'd slipped out of his flight suit and walked unnoticed through the crowd. He climbed the metal stairs outside Miles's aircraft hangar and walked into the giant, glass-walled living room above it. The room was crowded with the casino owner's friends and family. At the sight of Gus, Miles led an impromptu cheer amongst the guests, many of whom were watching a college football game on the large, flat screen television and noshing on a lavish buffet and open bar. Gus was forced into five minutes of awkward handshakes and slaps on the back from the gathered crowd, including John Ramos, the casino's general manager, and the largest gathering of whales that Gus had ever seen. These were the big spenders in the casino whom Gus often took for backseat rides in Miles's gold-painted Texan Lucky Strike—one of the perks extended to these high-rollers, who thought nothing of dropping $200,000 on craps in one night.

This group had been hanging out in Miles's hangar penthouse all week, being whisked over in the casino's small fleet of gold SUV limousines from their Mother Lode suites. Several of them wore XXL replicas of Gus's own flight suit—he realized Miles was not going to be happy that he didn't have his on right now.

Sitting alone in a corner of the room was Greg Calvino, owner and financier of *Wild Horse*, five-time defending champion and one of the planes Gus would be facing again in the finals. Calvino saw Gus looking at him and smirked, raising his highball glass in a mock toast to his victory.

Miles rose from the plush, theater-style seat in the center of the room and walked toward Gus, pumping his hand with a young man's grip and announcing to the room, "Folks, you'll have to excuse us—we have to work on our winning strategy." Miles ushered Gus down a short hallway and opened a door to a small, well-appointed office. Gus had never been inside any of the penthouse's private rooms before. Miles pulled the door shut behind them, walking around an antique desk, upon which sat a detailed wooden model of *One Tough Mother*.

Miles grabbed a small white envelope from the desk.

"Have a seat."

Gus sat in one of the two guest chairs facing the desk and smoothed the legs of his trousers with both hands.

"Gus, we've never had this opportunity before, and I'd like to personally thank you for getting us here."

"Thank you, Miles. We'd never have the plane to do it without all of your support."

"Aw. All I do is throw money at Dean and tell him to make her faster. Of course, once she gets airborne it's all up to you."

"Well Miles, there's a lot of luck involved."

The two men continued their mutually admiring banter and discussed the reasons why the plane was performing so well this year. Miles was thrilled that *Mother* was prepped and ready after the day's qualifier had put them into the Trophy Race for the first time ever. He held the envelope over the desk, presenting it to Gus.

Inside were twenty hundred-dollar bills.

"Miles, thank you. I..." Being handed a wad of cash like he'd just mown his boss's lawn or washed his car made Gus squirm.

"Gus," Miles continued, "I know you saw Greg Calvino out there. We were watching you race. Things got a little heated between us and I shot my mouth off..."

Miles's famous temper had cost him many things over the years, including three marriages. "...somehow I committed myself to a bet on the final heat and, well, there's a hell of a lot on the line here, Gus."

"Like what?"

"Like *Mother*. Plus the ground crew and a six-figure payout."

"Jesus!"

Gus felt a huge fist squeeze his vital organs. If the plane was lost, no pilot would be needed to fly it. Miles had shouted out his bet mid-race without a thought about how it might affect his employees. Now, Gus had to win. Otherwise, he might as well hang up his flight suit, kiss Lindsay goodbye one last time and ship her off to her mother for good as he spent the rest of his flyable years crisscrossing the country, shuttling corporate suits into regional airports.

"I don't need to tell you how great this would be for the Mother Lode, Gus."

"No."

"Good. Then let's get out there tomorrow and take it all the way!"

"I'll do my damndest, Miles."

"That's all I can ask."

The two men shook hands across the desk and Miles opened the door for Gus. In the hallway, Miles grabbed him by the arm.

"Gus."

"Yeah?"

"Don't ever leave the pits again without your goddamned flight suit on."

Dean and the rest of the crew were working late that night when Gus finally returned to the pits. The new liquid cooling system had been giving the guys fits. The guys pulled the engine, drained and changed all colors of viscous fluids. As long as the engine stayed together and Gus could pick his way through the pack in the final, they had one of the best planes running this year.

There was too much to do during race week for Gus to drive all the way home and back every day. He slept in the master bedroom of the team's motor coach that resembled the luxury bus of a touring rock band. The rig had a pop-out living room with plush carpet, leather furniture, and a full kitchen. The master bathroom had a round glass shower and the king-sized bed was the most comfortable that Gus had ever slept on. He had no excuse to be tired for any of his races, though he rarely caught more than two hours of sleep at a time in his anxious, adrenaline-fueled state.

He was making coffee at six the next morning when he heard a loud knock on the door of the coach. John Ramos stood on the small aluminum step. Gus and John had a real affinity for one another, and while both were beholden to Miles Jay for their generous salaries and benefits, they had also allied in the past to convince him to shelve some of his more bizarre ideas.

Several Indian mega-casinos had recently been built in the Sacramento Valley and were cutting into the profits of some of the Reno properties, including the Mother Lode. While John came up with a slew of clever marketing and promotions ideas that would help stanch the flow of the casino's losses, Miles wanted to exact revenge with a prominent publicity stunt.

Miles asked Gus to lead his squadron of planes and a crew of hired pilots down to the Raincloud Valley Resort and Casino and buzz the brand new ten-story hotel while people were flocking from the parking lot for the Neil Diamond concert during the grand opening. Miles even had the casino marketing department design mockups of a new paint scheme for *One Tough Mother* and three of his T-6 Texans. Instead of the sexed-up Rosie the Riveter nose art and the gold nugget tail logos, each plane was to fly the blue and yellow insignia of the U.S. 7th Cavalry. Painted in four-foot-tall letters on each fuselage were the words "Custer's Air Force." Miles even wanted to strap dummy bombs under the wings and fit each plane with smoke generators for their simulated bombing runs on what he called "that goddamned Indian village."

Neither Gus nor John ever wanted to butt heads with Miles Jay, but together they convinced him that the negative backlash of his treasured California customers would not make all of the free publicity worth it. He cursed his frequent gamblers as a bunch of "pansy politically correct Indian lovers," but finally conceded.

"Miles is very enthusiastic about your chances this year, Gus." John smiled.

"Yeah. I got that impression."

"I know this puts a lot of pressure on you, and I know what that can be like. How can I help?"

"Keep Miles off my back for the next couple days, and make sure Dean and the crew get whatever they need."

"Dean and the guys are already well taken care of. I'll do my best to keep Miles out of your hair, but you know that he wants to win this thing…*this year*."

John told Gus that if Gus placed in the top two, Miles might be willing to let him retire from the pressure of competition and become the "resident legend" at the Mother Lode, resuming his glad-handing PR duties without having to worry about the racing. Nothing sounded better to Gus, although he knew that if he didn't deliver, Miles would have no plane for him to show off.

Zoey Bishop lived with her mother, her sister Claire, and her one-year-old niece in one of the forty-year-old tract houses that had gone up outside the gates of what was once the Stead Airfield. She was supposed to be visiting with her dad across town, but she had blown him off and decided to have some friends over. Her mom was checking at the grocery store up the street, the baby was at daycare, and Claire was waiting tables at the Outpost Truck Stop Diner; Zoey had the house to herself. It was the final day of the air races, and her friends Savannah and Kate were excited to get smashed, lie out in the sun, and watch the planes roar low over the desert of Zoey's backyard.

She'd waited for her mom to leave for the store, promising

to take the bus downtown and transfer to the line that led to her dad's. As the sputtering of her mom's Toyota became muffled by the closing garage door, Zoey spied through the window, making sure her mom's little car was well on its way up the road. Satisfied, she went into the garage and pulled one of her dad's old deer-hunting tarps from the top of a cooler containing a twelve pack of cheap beer she'd bribed Claire to buy her in exchange for babysitting her niece. Zoey choked down a lump of guilt as she went back inside to get her phone.

Mom GONE, she texted, *come ovr.*

Zoey sat at the kitchen table and watched her Rottweiler, Max, sniffing at the back fence. A flight of biplanes buzzed past in the distance; the dog's massive head swung skyward and cocked to the side.

Her phone buzzed against the oak tabletop.

OMW.

Zoey smiled. She grabbed plastic ice trays from the freezer and emptied both into the cooler of beer, refilling them in the kitchen sink before sliding them back into their cool, white slots. The process always reminded her of the sliding drawers in morgues on the forensic cop shows Claire and Mom liked to watch after work.

Gus climbed up the small ladder into his cockpit. He'd never made it to the Trophy Race before. This was what Miles Jay had spent millions of dollars on over the years. Gus tried his best to treat it as just another day at work. He picked his way through the preflight checklist, plugged his helmet cord into the radio, and gave John a thumbs-up. With a shudder, the propeller began spinning, and he eased *One Tough Mother* onto the taxiway. He took off third and followed *Wild Horse,* climbing skyward off the end of the runway and banking right over Highway 395 and up toward Peavine Mountain looming to the west. Gus played with the pitch of the propeller and the fuel mixtures until he felt everything was just the way he wanted it. Soon, the rest of the planes joined them high over Peavine, and the radio from the pace jet began giving each pilot instructions, lining them up for their charge toward the starting line. Gus's muscles were tense: he was clenching his sphincter and fighting an acidic bubble of bile that longed to erupt from his esophagus and into his helmet. Twice, he chewed back a burning slime that tasted of scrambled eggs, coffee, and vomit.

Once the starter was satisfied with the positions of the aircraft, he led them toward the course and pulled up and into a hard left-hand turn, calling over his radio, "Gentlemen, you have a race."

The other pilots wasted no time jockeying for position. *Wild Horse*'s left wing slid over the top of Gus's right one and sliced toward his canopy. The pilot's head turned to stare at him through the two layers of Plexiglas before the larger P-51 slid ahead and banked hard to the left. With no room to follow suit, Gus had to back off the throttle as he found himself looking straight at *Wild Horse*'s vertical stabilizer, now centered in his line of sight and pulling away. Altitude would allow him a little extra potential energy that could be turned into speed once they began rounding pylons. He eased the nose of the plane up above *Wild Horse*'s tail and watched as the other plane gained more distance, now ahead by half a football field and about thirty feet below him. This put *Wild Horse* in Gus's blind spot, which meant that *Mother* had to work without being able to see her competition. The mass of planes screamed down the Chute and onto the course.

The three girls walked through the kitchen in their bikinis and stepped through the door into Zoey's garage. Kate and

Zoey grabbed the ends of an aluminum extension ladder and propped it against the roof. The backyard was packed dirt and weeds and smelled of dog shit thanks to Max, who had free reign of the yard since Zoey's mom wouldn't let him in the house. Zoey climbed up first, scrambling onto the roof, setting the beer down, and turning to grab two towels from Kate, who followed her up the ladder. Savannah climbed up last, clutching a bottle of rum she'd pilfered that morning from her own house, and a silver reflective space blanket they had found in the garage. The three girls spread out the blanket and towels so they were facing the sun and the racecourse, and Zoey and Kate lay down on their backs. Savannah smiled down at the girls and reached around her back, unclasping her bikini top.

"Are you crazy, Savannah? We've got neighbors, you know."

"Nobody can see us up here, Zoey. Besides, they're just tits."

Shit. Zoey had never seen Savannah with her top off, except for sideways glances in the locker room during volleyball. *Those aren't just tits. They're what every guy in school would die just to see. They're* breasts.

The girls giggled as Savannah settled down on the silver blanket, pulling her sunglasses up to her forehead to look at her friends.

"Come on you guys—this way you don't get any tan lines. What're you afraid of?"

Kate took the rum bottle from Savannah, took a big swig, and laughed, removing her top and tossing it aside.

"Kate!" Zoey couldn't believe the girls were topless on *her* roof. While Savannah's were big, perfect, and tan, Kate's were four shades lighter than the rest of her body. She looked like she was wearing a white bikini top with a pair of faux rubies stitched on, one to the front of each cup.

Zoey stood in front of her two topless friends, her arms crossed in front of her B-cups as Kate and Savannah whooped like drunken frat boys. She could hear the bee drone engines of the planes starting to round the pylons.

"Come on, Zoey! We're going home if you're gonna be a little bitch about it." Savannah smiled and grabbed her own breasts, shaking them as she squinted and stuck her tongue out. Zoey paused, then pulled at the polyester bow at the back of her neck. Despite the warmth of the sun on her exposed breasts, she shivered and rolled over to the safety of her stomach.

"I'll tan my back first," she said.

Kate laughed, and Savannah proclaimed the roof as their own "white trash Riviera." They passed the bottle back and forth until it was half empty.

Gus stayed above *Wild Horse* around the first two pylons. This put him tight to the inside on the hard-banked left-hand turns. Still, the Mustang had a slight lead on Gus, and although *Mother* held the inside, he didn't have the line to slip past without risking cutting a pylon. If any of the judges stationed at the base of each pole could see any part of Gus's plane through the center of the barrel mounted atop it, they would call a cut pylon, and *Mother* would incur an eighteen-second time penalty. As the planes leveled off on the backside of the course, Gus looked for the best spot to pass the flying checkered cab. He sighted the best angle of attack and looked to the horizon to find a landmark on which to line up the pass, which he figured would be in lap seven or eight. There were a handful of small houses and a few trailers ahead. A silver flash streaked in through his canopy off the roof of the house closest to the course. Whatever it was, a solar panel or sheet metal roof flashing, he had his landmark—he would stay on the tail of the lead plane until one of the last laps, then line up with the silver reflection and make his pass.

With his landmarks established, Gus focused on everything

inside his cockpit. The oil pressure was right where it should be, and the engine temperature was not yet into the red—Dean's last-minute improvements to the cooling system seemed to be paying off. On the third and fourth laps, Gus played with *Wild Horse*, feigning several pass attempts on the long straightaway that led past the grandstands and into the home pylon. It always thrilled the crowd when planes raced close together, especially when they roared along, wingtip to wingtip, in front of the bleachers. Gus checked behind him and saw that he and the Mustang had a comfortable lead on the rest of the field—it was a two-plane race for the gold.

On lap six, a voice cracked over Gus's headset: "Race 32 has a Mayday!" He looked over his left shoulder and saw *Baron VR*, three pylons behind, level off and turn wide away from the course, smoke trailing behind the aircraft.

"Roger. Understand Mayday Race 32. Winds are fifteen knots from the southwest." Race Control's disembodied voice was calm and authoritative in the headset. Gus stayed on course and attuned himself to the developing situation on the radio. The German fighter had lost power; his propeller spun, impotent, in front of the gliding plane. The pilot would be making a dead-stick landing. They would not stop the race in order to get him on the ground.

The red plane drifted out of Gus's field of vision as he headed onto the back straightaway, setting his bearing on the starburst reflection from the roof of the house just off the course.

"Tower, *Baron VR* on the ground. Request recovery vehicle. Gear damaged, propeller sheared." The pilot sounded eerily calm, considering the plane had broken a landing wheel and nosed into the tarmac, shattering the $25,000 propeller.

"Roger, *Baron*. Crash team en route."

Gus focused on the planes still airborne. *Wild Horse* seemed to have a little extra horsepower left, and Gus could sense the

P-51 widening its lead by a few feet. He eased his throttle forward to keep pace and climbed another twenty feet. He could use the added altitude for a bit more speed when he took his pass on the next lap. Again, he found the bright beacon off above the sagebrush. He committed to his pass on the next revolution. Gus could see the black and yellow checkered wing slide under his own forward-swept right one, almost half of it disappearing as the Mustang's cockpit edged closer to his own. *Wild Horse* was tightening his line and wasn't going to let Gus pass him on the inside of any of the pylons. Gus had to fight the stick in his hand as *Mother* started buffeting in the vortex created by the two planes so close together, their enormous propeller blades cutting into the thin air of the mile-high altitude. Gus let *Wild Horse* push him up close to pylon five, and on the next straightaway he found his glinting landmark and made his move.

Gus shoved the throttle all the way forward. The needles on the engine temperature and oil pressure gauges shot into the red wedge painted on their white dials. *Mother's* wings swayed in the turbulent air, and the G-forces of the turn pushed Gus into his seat. The blood pooled in his legs and his field of vision narrowed. A thick black border pushed in from all sides as he squinted, keeping his course aligned with the silver flash. He prayed that the engine would hold. But it wasn't the engine that failed him. Centrifugal forces worked at the modified airframe, and, without warning, *One Tough Mother's* left wing folded up, then separated from the fuselage like a well-done drumstick pulled from a turkey carcass.

"Race 88 Mayday" were the last words Gus Shipley ever said.

Zoey felt the warmth of camaraderie and alcohol, as well as the sun on her exposed skin, as she and the girls rated the senior boys on various attributes. Eventually, her modesty melted in a puddle of rum and beer, and she was soon flat on her back, watching the sun paint colorful splotches on the insides of her eyelids.

It was Kate who noticed the gold and white plane veer hard off course and then break apart. What an odd thing to see the massive wing separate from the plane in midair. That tiny thing flying toward them didn't look large enough, or real enough, to contain a human being. Dulled by the warm buzz of alcohol, all she could manage was a choked, "Oh my God!"

Zoey and Savannah turned to watch the one-winged plane, traveling just shy of five hundred miles an hour, spinning wildly on its horizontal axis—the still-attached right wing now vertical like the fin of some aerial shark. One hundred yards from Zoey's back fence, *Mother* plowed into the sagebrush, kicking up a cloud of dust and debris that disappeared into a fireball and, seconds later, a mini mushroom cloud of black smoke.

The girls screamed as pieces of sand, rock, and airplane rained down on the roof. The heavy engine of the plane skidded across the scrub and sage, grinding across a rocky shelf in a shower of sparks and coming to rest twenty feet shy of the fence while the cockpit slid further across the ground, shedding pieces of aluminum, Plexiglas, and Gus Shipley. The firewall and instrument panel plowed through the thin fence boards. Charred chunks of airplane and pilot smoldered amongst weeds and large piles of Rottweiler shit. A piece of wing hit the legs of the ladder with a metallic clang. The atmosphere became heavy with an eerie silence, broken by the sobs of the three girls huddled in a beach towel. Zoey felt wetness on her left breast and noticed blood trickling from a tiny wound just below her nipple. A small piece of machined metal had pierced her, its tiny, brushed-aluminum end protruding from her chest. She pulled it out and winced at the clean slit that would remain forever: a small, white, crescent moon on her breast.

Zoey looked across the desert toward the pylons and the grandstands packed with spectators, their abstract shapes elongated and dancing in the shimmering, superheated air.

All at once, the air came alive with a cacophony of sirens.

AROUND THE BEND

Patrick Branson was awake at four in the morning. In the darkness, he found a tenuous thought. Some synapse long gone cold had fired back up—or maybe two mental wires, insulation worn away from years of jangling inside his head, had crossed, sending a brief electric impulse to a dormant part of his brain. In a rare, clear moment, he knew what he was going to do that day. It—the train—became his sole objective.

He stepped across the oval rug on the bedroom floor. On a chair lay a blue nylon sweat suit. Pants on top, jacket underneath, socks—not balled together but flat on the chair back. Patrick turned to a small closet, in whose dark corner hung an old set of railroad work clothes. He laid the working-man's uniform out on the unmade bed: blue chino work shirt, denim overalls, and an oilcloth jacket for chilly mornings. He could not find a pair of work boots and, instead, slipped on a pair of white sneakers and fastened them with two Velcro straps.

He studied the framed photos someone had lined up across the top of the bureau. The faces—many happy, some black and white—were unrecognizable. The smiles looked sincere, the eyes, through shape and color, spoke of family relationships. Daughters, mothers, siblings. Patrick didn't know whose.

Among the large brass picture frames stood a wooden box with a hinged lid. Patrick opened it and pulled out a gold pocket watch, which he tucked into the jacket's large chest pocket. He quietly moved through the house, finding his way through the kitchen and out the back door. He was on the road by 5:00 a.m., plenty of time to catch the 6:15 from Verdi.

At 7:00 a.m., Frances Dunn's alarm chirped. She slapped the button on top of the clock and nestled back into the warmth of her covers. She strained to hear sounds of movement in the house below. It was Saturday—no work today, at least not any she would get paid for. Her three charges were still. Soundless. Frances stretched across her large bed and inhaled several times. She kicked her legs over the side and staggered to the bathroom to empty her bladder. She was still awash in sleep when she zipped up her ankle-length robe and headed down to the kitchen to cook her father's breakfast. At 7:15 a.m., she crossed the kitchen and rapped a knuckle against his bedroom door. By this time every morning, he was sitting in the recliner next to his bed listening to the big band CD she had put in the clock radio, set to play every morning at 6:00. She smiled when she heard the brassy tones of a horn section muffled through the hollow wood panel of the door. No doubt he was enraptured with Benny Goodman and unaware of her quiet knocks. When she opened the door and saw the empty bed and folded sweat suit on the chair, her throat tightened and her legs felt as if she was standing on a moving bus, unable to reach the grab handles overhead.

"Dad? Dad!"

He was not in the adjacent half bath, not anywhere else in the house. At 7:20 a.m., she dialed 9-1-1.

Patrick crept along the street. Every thought was a battle for recognition, an agonizing attempt to make something fit. His muddled memory flipped like a deck of cards.

He squinted at the intense morning light, raising a gnarled hand to his brow. Stark illumination blurred the identities of objects and places. The sun, low on the horizon, seemed to be pointed right at him, a lone headlight bearing down, blinding him with its intensity. He remembered the train. He'd have to hurry.

Ambling down the sidewalk that rolled away from his feet in smooth curbs, he felt he was circling. All of the little two-story houses in Riverview had the same porches and driveways and front doors. All were painted shades of light brown, differing only by degrees of sunlight and shadow. All of the streets were named after something. Maybe they were countries. Or states. Rivers. The streets were all the names of rivers.

Patrick had wandered up half a dozen semicircular cul de sacs (had he walked up some of them more than once?) when he heard a train whistle rolling through the humid morning air. He worked himself along the sidewalks until he came to a break in the split rail fence. Someone had already worn a trail through the hedges that bordered the group of houses standing shoulder to shoulder. The footpath led into the thickness of undergrowth. Leafy shade overhead cooled him as he wound for a few dozen feet through the small forest. He lost all bearing and stood on the path, unsure. He felt himself weeping; small sobs cut off his breath and shook his body. He raised his arms to his chest to hug himself, and his right hand felt a hard bulge in the jacket pocket. He reached in under the canvas flap and felt a metal disc, warmed by his body. A small chain was attached to one end. He pulled it from the pocket and saw the gleam of polished gold, bright even in the trees' shadows. A tiny button flipped open the pocket watch; it was twenty past six. He heard another blast from a train whistle. It was not far away. He turned, followed the trail in the direction of the sound. A diesel engine rumbled low in the distance.

The emergency dispatcher's flat, disembodied voice seemed to be judging Frances.

"Has he gone missing before, ma'am?"

"No, no. This has never happened before."

"Have you thoroughly checked every room of the house?"

"Yes. Of course. I wouldn't have called you if…"

"I know this is very stressful, ma'am. I have to ask these questions."

Frances closed her eyes and grabbed a handful of her duvet cover, crinkling the even pattern of small, pink roses.

"Have the two of you been arguing?" The dispatcher's androgynous tone was relentless in its calm.

"No! Look, I've searched everywhere. The booklet says that timing is everything when someone wanders off—are you sending anyone to help me find my father?"

"They're on the way. Would you like me to stay on the phone until they arrive?"

"No. Thank you."

Frances hung up and heard the shuffle of small feet in the hallway. Peter stood in her bedroom doorway. Eddie was close behind, clutching his older brother's arm and rubbing half-closed eyes. The boys must've been awakened by her yelling for Patrick, and she wondered what they'd heard of the phone conversation. Eight-year-old Peter was ready to set out with a flashlight to go out and find his grandfather.

"Boys, Poppy left the house this morning. The police are looking for him. We need to stay here and wait for him. He'll be back soon."

"Did you forget to set the door alarm, Mom?" Peter was being practical, but his words stabbed at her. The piercing yelp of the back door alarm hadn't woken her, and while searching the house, she found she'd forgotten to set it the night before.

Frances sent Eddie back to his room to get dressed. She told

Peter the best thing was to stay put in case Patrick returned home on his own or a neighbor called to report seeing Patrick walk by a breakfast nook window in the rising light of dawn.

Frances and Peter, each dressed in a sweat suit, marched down the stairs and entered the kitchen side by side. Frances pulled a manila folder from the drawer of a built-in desk next to the kitchen. There were several recent color photographs of her father inside, along with a faxable sheet of paper with his name and a description so stereotypical that Frances chuckled—it read like a bank robbery report:

Name: (First) Patrick, (Middle) Edward, (Last) Branson. Height: 5'10". Weight: 165. Hair: Gray. Eyes: Blue.

Eddie went back to his room to look for his best Poppy-finding stuff. He kept on his camouflaged pajama bottom shorts and pulled his brother's pirate skull T-shirt over his pajama top. He found the furry hat with the animal tail stuck on the back that his dad brought him from a trip and pulled it over his messy hair. He remembered the red binoculars on his dresser that had a string to hang around his neck. He would use those to find Poppy. He really liked his grandpa, even though Poppy didn't ever remember his name. His grandpa always played along with his imagination games, even when Peter wouldn't. Eddie dug through the piles of clothes in his closet and looked under his and Peter's beds, in case Poppy was hiding in their room. He checked the hallway toy box and the closet where Mom kept their bed blankets, then threw aside the shower curtain in their bathroom—where Eddie always hid when he and Peter played hide-and-seek. He searched every Poppy-sized place in the house before he went downstairs to find his flip-flops, so he could hunt for Poppy outside.

Patrick made his way through thick brush. The trail spilled out onto a wide dirt swath. At eye-level, on the crown of a gravel ribbon, was a rusted brown rail. He climbed up the pebbled berm and lifted one leg, then the other, stepping over the first rail. He stood with one foot each on the thick, creosote-covered ties and listened for the boiling sound of the oncoming train. He could feel the thickening air pushing ahead of it like an invisible wall, even while the train was out of sight around a bend in the tracks. He flipped open the pocket watch and checked the dials: the train was running on time. He pinched the watch shut and placed it back in the pocket of the coat. His hands were unable to secure the two buttons on the flap.

"Judy, Dad is gone."

Frances waited through the wrenching pause before her sister's voice startled her with its sudden volume.

"He's dead?"

"No. He got out of the house this morning. The back-door alarm wasn't set. The police are looking for him."

Frances watched a galaxy of dusty stars spiral in a warm, ruddy beam of the rising sun as it cut through the kitchen window and lit the varnished brown pane of her dining room table.

"Goddammit, Frances. How could you just let him walk out of—?"

"Judy. Please. Just come over."

"You knew this was a possibility. The alarm can't just be left off. The lock should never be undone. This wouldn't have happened at a home."

"Please!" Frances's voice cracked. She wiped her eyes with the long sleeve of her robe.

"I'll be there in a half hour."

Frances walked to the stove, lit the burner, and filled a steel kettle in the sink. While the kettle hammered to a boil atop the blue flame, Frances opened the refrigerator and removed a dozen eggs, a package of pre-cooked sausages, a sleeve of bacon, two sticks of butter, and a large plastic jug of maple syrup.

She crouched on her haunches and pulled a black cast-iron griddle from a lower cabinet, placing it over the two front burners next to the kettle, which was already building a head of steam.

Peter walked into the kitchen, Eddie a few steps behind. Frances cracked two eggs at a time on the glass lip of a measuring cup, sliding the viscous yellow orbs onto a layer of butter already bubbling brown on the shimmering surface of the griddle. She added six strips of bacon, then turned her back to the sizzling mass of meat and eggs to begin the pancake batter.

"Your grandfather will be home soon." She stirred thick, chalky mix in a large bowl on the kitchen island, then slid a wooden spoon on the rim of a bowl, skinning it of batter.

"Did the police find him?" Peter stepped further from the griddle, now launching a caustic spittle of bacon grease and butter in tiny, searing pearls that arced toward his bare arms, stinging him.

"No. Not yet." She turned, spatula in hand, and flipped the eggs, now perfect yellow irises staring up at the range hood. "But he will be back before breakfast is finished."

The kettle rattled and shrilled a high-pitched, steamy whine. With her free hand, Frances turned the burner off and opened the small flap-valve on the spout, unleashing thin steam.

Eddie climbed onto his chair at the table. The room filled with the savory scent of frying animal fat and the maple sweetness of syrup emanating from the neck of the jug, warming in a saucepan of water on a back burner.

"Sit down, Peter." Frances gestured with the greasy spatula.

"Poppy will be back. I promise."

Peter pulled a gallon of milk from the refrigerator's door. He grabbed two plastic cups from a lower cabinet and set them on the table, one in front of his little brother and the other at his own place at the head of the table. He poured milk into both cups and returned the plastic jug to the refrigerator, never once looking at his mother.

Twenty-five minutes later, Judith arrived to a community-sized pancake breakfast like they held at the firehouse on the Fourth of July. Stacks of flapjacks warmed in the oven. A pitcher of orange juice flanked a platter of glistening bacon, two dozen sausage links, a pan full of eggs, and a plate of wheat toast. Judith was only interested in the pot of freshly brewed coffee.

"The police having breakfast here later?" Judith winked. Frances didn't respond.

"I think Dad will find his way back just following the smell of fried meat," Judith tried again.

This time Frances smiled. "Yeah, one thing Dad didn't forget was that he loved bacon."

"How long has he been out?" Judith looked hard at Frances over the rim of her coffee mug and took a long sip.

"I don't know. He was already gone when I woke up." Frances looked at her boys at each end of the table, both eating pancakes soaking in syrup.

Judith took another long sip of coffee and placed her mug on the table in front of her, gripping it with both hands. "He may never come back, Frances. Not alive. If he gets out to a busy road...or has a fall."

Frances rose from her chair. "Shut up, Judith! Shut up and don't blame me. He's coming home!"

Patrick was on the familiar pebbled gravel of a railbed. So much forgotten. Names. Faces. But this he knew. Tracks. Signals. The feel of the raised levy of pebbles beneath his feet. He was on a mainline that branched into a nearby siding. To his right, the track ran to the horizon in a straight section, flanked by industrial buildings and a frontage road. To his left, the track ran straight for thirty yards, then disappeared in a sweeping turn that swallowed the steel ribbons and creosote-filled ties back into the wooded greenery he had emerged from. This was not the place he'd envisioned when he awoke this morning, but it would do. He turned to his left. The locomotive bore down on him, still out of sight around the turn.

As the diesel engine's throbs became more sensations than sounds, he saw the train round the bend, thin black smoke rising behind the twin headlights, bright even in the morning sunlight. He shuffled his feet and squared himself between the rails, finding footing on a crosstie. The locomotive crew must have seen him—he heard a series of hard, short blasts on the air horn as the machine charged at him like a sooty bull. The sound of the horn, the vibration of the engine, the smell of the diesel exhaust, the grind of the brakes, and the glare of the headlights merged into a single, sensory experience for a moment before his beloved beast smashed through his willing body. His arms and legs slapped the metal plate on the machine's front, and his torso seemed to liquefy as Patrick's body flew backward.

The call came over the sheriff's car radio at 8:27 a.m.: a robotic female voice whose amplification chopped the words with static. Deputy John Kreiger caught a glimpse of his own boyish face and close-cropped sandy hair in his driver's mirror and saw himself grimace. He knew that the "elderly white male" who had been hit on the freight siding near the rail yard was the wandering grandfather he was looking for. He had hoped to find the old guy walking on the bike path that curved past the housing complex into the neighborhoods that followed the Truckee River's shallow meander downtown. Now he had to go back to the daughter's house, knock on the door, and tell her that her father was dead, his body now a shattered counterpart to his fragmented brain, both smashed into pieces by a slow-moving freight train. He turned his cruiser around and sped to the track's closest access point. He could hear the thrumming of the idling diesel long before he made it to the clearing and saw the great machine. Its crew was pacing in small, worried circles. Halfway down the length of the train, a pair of shoes lay askew, side-by-side. Their straps were fastened. One of the railroad men was across the tracks, bent over a shape covered with a heavy canvas jacket. Gravel crunched underfoot as the young patrolman walked to the body, nodded to the man bent above it, and removed the impromptu winding sheet.

The old man was grotesquely bent. Both shoulders had been dislocated and both clavicles broken so that the arms appeared to be mounted to the same side of the body. One leg had broken in so many pieces that it curled all the way to the top of the head. The thick denim fabric of the overalls held the leg in place—the sinew and human fibers had released their hold on the appendage. The head had detached from the spine, but the flexible, wrinkled skin of the neck had remained intact. Kreiger remembered seeing this condition, called internal decapitation, at a car accident. Despite the angle of the head, the old man's face appeared undamaged. The corpse looked like a sleeping marionette whose strings had been cut.

The boys had been outside for over an hour, searching the backyard and the cul de sac out front. She could hear them every two or three minutes, Peter shouting, "Grandpa!" and Eddie yelling behind him, "Pah-pee!"

Frances and Judith sat at the oak dining table, each with a mug in front of them, the coffee and the tea long gone cold.

Eddie barged in the front door in a gleeful frenzy. "Mom! Aunt Judith! Come here!"

The seed of dread that Frances had clenched in her gut all morning rose to her throat as she made it to the open door where Peter stood between two olive-drab uniformed Washoe County sheriff's deputies on her front porch.

"Mrs. Dunn? May we come in?"

The afternoon of her father's death slipped beneath a flood of minutiae. There were questions for the sisters to answer from the police, personal items of their father's to claim. Forms to fill out and sign. She remembered holding her boys in her arms and tearfully explaining that Poppy wasn't coming home. Eddie nodded. Peter cried, which made Eddie cry.

The boys fell asleep late that night, in Frances's bed with the television mumbling across the room. Frances took a long look at their sweet faces, sliding in and out of focus in the cold, blue strobe of TV commercials. She made her way back downstairs where Judith sat at the kitchen table.

"Why do you think Dad wandered off, Frances?"

"I think he was trying to go to work. I think that part of his brain still remembered his old routine."

"You think he was trying to get *on* that train?" Judith rubbed her temples and fixed her gaze on her sister. "Frances, I don't think you were listening to the police. Dad stood *in front* of that train—he knew it would kill him. He was done. He woke up in his little room, looked around, and then made one final, conscious decision."

Unbelievable. The mere mention of suicide was absurd. *Dad was a good Catholic. He'd never get to see Mom again. Not if he'd committed suicide.* Frances took a few calming breaths.

"Judith." She searched for the right words in what would be the last conversation she would have with her sister. "You think he just woke up that morning, recognized the picture of his wife, his kids, himself—and decided to throw himself in front of a freight train?"

"No. I think he woke up that morning, *didn't* recognize the pictures on his dresser, didn't recognize his face in the bathroom mirror, and only remembered the trains. At least it gave him something familiar to throw himself in front of."

Frances rose from the table, set her mug on its chipped, faded surface, and glared at her sister.

"I'm sorry, Judith. I'm sorry Dad's dead. I'm sorry the goddamn alarm was off. I'm sorry you didn't get to put him in a home. Blame me. I deserve it. But don't ever, *ever* talk about Dad like that again." She turned and headed for her bedroom. She flicked the light switch at the bottom of the stairs out of habit and left her sister sitting in the dark.

In the car on the way home from Patrick's funeral mass at St. Elizabeth's Catholic Church, Peter asked, "Mom, do you think Grandpa will go to heaven?"

Frances had to uncoil her tongue, having spent the last hour across the aisle from Judith without speaking or glancing at her. "Of course, sweetheart. He joined Grandma there. Why would you even ask that question?"

"Mrs. Hawkins told us in church school that if you kill yourself, you can't go to heaven. She said people who commit suicide go to hell."

Frances gripped the steering wheel and felt her foot mash down on the accelerator. She swerved into the left lane to keep from bashing a slower car in front of her.

"Poppy is not in hell!" Frances began crying. The road was

a wet blur, and she moved her foot to the brake pedal and relaxed her grip on the wheel. *Judith.* Her sister had poisoned the boys' minds not only against her, but against their deceased grandfather.

"I don't care what your teacher says, and I damn well don't care what your aunt tells you! Poppy did not kill himself. He was just trying to get on that train and do his job."

Peter slouched in his seat and stared at his knees. Eddie looked over at his brother and aped his pensive silence. The family, just the three of them now, rode home to the sound of their tires on asphalt and Frances's chuffed breathing as she sobbed for her disintegrating family—a husband gone off to another life, a father dead, a sister estranged.

The house found a new routine. The boys had taken weeks to adjust to their grandfather's absence but were now comfortable to explore the artifacts of his railroad days, turning on the big band CDs when they visited his room. Because of visitation rights granted to her ex-husband, the shop manager at the Outpost Truck Stop, she was bound to this place, unable to take the boys and move away. The frequent blasts of the air horns on the diesel locomotives that rolled through town at all hours stabbed through her numb cocoon and split open old wounds. When the keening of the freight trains penetrated the night and entered her bedroom, she would often imagine her father standing next to the tracks—one arm raised to hail the passing freight, hoping the engineer would slow it so that he could swing aboard in one smooth motion, a practiced maneuver that was second nature to someone who had worked his whole life on the railroad. Sometimes she would see him slip, stumbling over a raised tie between the rails or losing his footing on the gravel railbed. Her thoughts always returned to her dark bedroom and her present life before the train hit him. Not once did she imagine him how Judith described, standing steadily between the rails, arms at his side, watching the front of the locomotive approach until it met him squarely—its sheer mass and momentum unaffected by the tiny collision with an eminently moveable object.

LETDOWN

Michael Henry Galen was born August 17th. He weighed six pounds, four ounces. He was 19 inches long. Michael Henry Galen died in his sleep sometime during the night of September 23rd. Mary found him lying silent in his crib. She'd forever be ashamed to remember how glad she was for his silence that morning. He'd been fussy that night, and she fed and rocked the red-faced boy for hours until the delirium of exhaustion took hold.

When she turned on the silver airplane lamp, his tiny face and balled fists were periwinkle. His baby features were a portrait of peaceful sleep, but the chest of his sleeper did not rise and fall with the rapid breathing she'd become accustomed to.

Wayne had been able to sleep again for hours at a time after a few weeks without Michael in the house. When Wayne rolled onto his back and began snoring, Mary snuck down to the unfinished basement and pulled the electric breast pump from its hiding place behind a pile of cardboard boxes. She hadn't been able to let go of her body's last tangible maternal process, even though she felt she was betraying Wayne with her secret ritual, a ceremonial feeding of their lost child. The trumpet-shaped pump buzzed and tugged at her, and she cried as her ducts were emptied. She managed about four ounces from each side.

Mary placed the plastic bag of her warm, parchment-colored nourishment in the deep freezer under large bags of forgotten vegetables. There were already rows of other frozen milkings hidden away in the lower racks under Wayne's butcher-wrapped ground venison from his fall hunt. Today was to be her first time out of the house since she'd come back from the hospital to a nursery full of useless receiving blankets and layettes, a crib, and a diaper pail. Her mother had been pushing her to come to church and find *peace*. Mary and her husband hadn't been back to St. Elizabeth's since their wedding. Wayne had never been a churchgoer and had only gone through his conversion, attending marriage classes with Father del Rios, to please her parents. When she woke up this morning, the idea of being among a large group of people seemed comforting. And her mother had promised they could arrive late, sit toward the back, and leave after communion, slipping out before mass ended to avoid any awkward personal expressions of condolence.

Wayne would stay home and dismantle the nursery, something that needed doing before they sold the house. They couldn't bear strangers walking through Michael's room, now a mausoleum disguised as a nursery. St. Elizabeth's was supposed to give her peace, a sense of sanctuary and community. The parishioners had the decency to give her space.

During the homily, just as she was finding consolation in Father del Rios's commentary on Mark 10:13, an infant began crying in the back vestibule. Its mother spirited the baby away into the back of the church, into a side aisle or the crying room, but it was too late.

Mary felt a twinge deep in her belly, a tingle at her breasts. A prickle and then wetness, a slow trickle at first; the pearly liquid soaked into her bra and darkened her white blouse. She covered her chest with both forearms. By the time she reached the side door, it was difficult to tell whether the damp patches on her blouse were from milk or from briny tears that fell in rivulets on her breasts, still ignorantly swollen for her dead motherhood. Mary paused at the top of the steps leading down to the parking lot. Her mother caught up to her and grasped her arm just below the elbow. It had been snowing since they'd entered the church, and the parking lot and cars were coated three inches deep. Large, asymmetrical flakes fell.

Cold air hardened the milk staining the front of her blouse, and Mary wished she had brought a coat, not for warmth, but to disappear into as she and her mother made the long walk to the car. She could still hear the baby crying, if only in her memory, and the infant in the church and her own Michael wailed in unison, a duet of shrieks that tugged at her maternity and again sent milk flowing.

Her mother opened the passenger door and guided Mary to the seat. They drove into the storm, the children's cries blending with the harsh scrape of the wipers streaking across the freezing windshield of her mother's car.

DEADHEADING

The manufactured landscape of the Outpost Truck Stop parking lot held dozens of aluminum arroyos that throbbed with the staccato pings of a hundred diesel engines. The motors held back the freezing night, the drivers cocooned against the cold, lulled to sleep while burning the fuel that cut into their livelihood as they snored, nestled in their sleeping bags.

A space in the third row of the lot had room enough for two trucks, but Billy Donovan was not able to maneuver as precisely as most drivers. He always hunted for the biggest spot he could find—his truck always parked at odd angles from the rest of the rigs, the trailer often impeding one of the lanes leading to the diesel pumps. Parking stripes were often disregarded.

He clutched the table-flat steering wheel with both hands, ground into a lower gear, and cranked the machine into a jack-knifed turn as the metallic purple Peterbilt pulled to a stop. Many drivers kept their trucks as clean and detailed as they could, but Billy's truck was a garish, gleaming machine that he washed at least twice a week. The trailer captured the attention of highway drivers with its airbrushed mural of a wagon train crossing Donner Summit on the left side and a sunset over the Truckee Meadows on the right. Billy had seen many cars weaving near his trailer in his rearview mirrors, their drivers pulling alongside to gawk at the details on his rolling vistas.

Billy could tell the truck wasn't straight in the spot, but he was hungry, and tired of sitting in one place. A great hiss shot from below the cab, the brakes exhaling compressed air and locking the wheels in place. Snow started to fall in large flakes, and a dizzying pattern of cold dander appeared within the headlight beams; each crystal spun in its own vortex before disappearing into darkness at the edge of the cones of illumination.

"Lights off! Shift to neutral! Set parking brake! Logbook!" Billy's thick lips glistened with spittle. He grunted and tugged, releasing the tension of the seat belt across his massive girth, pulling on the nylon strap until there was enough slack to release the buckle. He grabbed a spiral-bound black book from between the two seats. For some drivers, the logbook was an afterthought at the end of a late night—for others it was a work of fiction that taxed the limits of its author's creativity. For Billy, it was a difficult but honest undertaking. To fill it out required both physical dexterity and a basic grasp of math. He had neither.

Each page was divided into a twenty-four-hour grid with four rows of hours: *Off Duty, Driving, Sleeper Berth* and *On Duty (Not Driving)*. With a small plastic ruler, Billy tried to draw a straight horizontal line across the rows according to the hours he drove, slept, loaded and spent off duty. He cursed several times as his sausage fingers struggled to hold the pencil and draw a straight line; he had to use a thick pink gum eraser several times. He finished his entry—four hours driving, eight off duty, four on duty (not driving) and eight in the sleeper—and zipped the book back into its nylon case. He opened the door of his cab and enjoyed the shock of cold air. He left the motor idling and climbed down onto the step mounted across the top of his left fuel tank—one of a pair of giant chrome saddlebags that protruded like silver outriggers on either side of the cab. As he took the last step toward the ground, his large, silver-plated belt buckle snagged on the top of the aluminum step. He kicked his legs, unable to find purchase on anything solid, and felt a sharp pain in his gut as his massive weight pressed down on the saucer-sized buckle, which stabbed into layers of soft fat. Cussing and grunting, he lifted himself up by the grab bar next to the door and reached along his soft underbelly until he was able to release himself. Already the moisture in his scruffy salt-and-pepper beard was beginning to freeze.

As he walked alongside his truck and down the parallel rows of rigs, Billy noticed his footprints in the light dusting of snow on the blacktop. In the narrow space between a car carrier and a flatbed, he lay on his back on the cool pavement, waving his arms and legs in a horizontal jumping jack. He closed his thick-lidded eyes and focused on the snow landing on his outstretched tongue. After several minutes, he stood to admire his black angel flanked in white. It made him think of Anise for a moment, and the paper bag of her pictures in his sleeper. He smiled.

Billy noticed steam coming out of his mouth. He pushed as much air out of his belly as he could, and watched as dragon puffs of smoke shot into the sky, backlit by the yellow parking lot lights. Soon it hurt to breathe the cold air, and he continued on his way to the coffee shop.

As he crossed the lot, several of the regulars greeted Billy as they headed in and out of the shop and café. He had as many different pet names as there were drivers.

"Good evening, Champ."

"Howdy, Cowboy."

"How's it goin', Wild Bill?"

"How's your peter built, Billy?"

That one always made him laugh. He knew it had something to do with both his truck and his pecker. He didn't get why it was funny, but the guys always chuckled, so he laughed along. Many of these drivers had let Billy spend time behind the wheels of their own rigs in the parking lot. They'd adopted the middle-aged, orphaned, retarded guy several years ago and had been collectively determined to help him pass his written and practical tests so he could get his CDL. He bought his rig with his mother's life insurance payout and had it delivered to the gravel overflow lot, where it sat in the guarded compound until he could legally drive it. The truckers, security guards, maintenance men, coffee shop waitresses and store employees loved having Billy around. He inspected their tires and tie-downs, and was always willing to help strap down a load, hold a flashlight or turn a wrench. He was a surrogate child for many long-haulers who didn't see their own sons and daughters for weeks at a time. They'd pay him a little cash to clean out their cabs after a long run, and he was the resident source of information when it came to the nearby Palomino Ranch Brothel, a favorite stopover for several of the road-weary men.

Jean was pouring coffee for another late-night customer at the counter when she saw Billy waddle in the door, grab the scattered sections of a newspaper from the hostess stand, and head to his favorite booth by the window.

"Billy! I've missed you, sweetheart."

"Hi, Jean. I'm hungry." Billy plopped onto the vinyl seat and pushed the formica table away from his girth.

Jean walked over, silver carafe in hand, and flipped over the ceramic white mug in front of Billy, filling it halfway. He lifted the ribbed glass cylinder of sugar and dumped a cascade into the coffee. Even at arm's length Jean could smell him—a funk of sour cabbage, rancid meat, and wet dog, all suspended in the sweat of a day laborer. She held a long breath, letting the retching feeling pass, and counted as he emptied five corrugated plastic containers of half and half into the coffee and whisked it with his spoon.

"I'll get your order in, honey. How was your drive?"

"Good. I'm tired. And hungry."

"I'm movin' as fast as this old lady can." She smiled and shuffled back into the kitchen and wrote out his ticket: scrambled eggs with cheese, side of bacon, side of ham, side of sausage, two buttermilk biscuits with gravy, hash browns, bowl of Fruit Loops, and a large glass of whole milk. The enormous man had an appetite, and he always ordered breakfast regardless of the time of day.

Billy sorted through the sections of the *Reno Gazette Journal* he'd grabbed on the way in and restacked them in his order of preference: Comics, Sports, TV Week, and the glossy, full-color advertisements for Wal Mart, Kohl's, Target and—his favorite—the Outdoor Superstore.

He was halfway through the funnies when Jean set his meal before him. The thin knobs of her wrist bones showed the strain of carrying his overloaded plates. He tossed the sections in a crumpled pile on the peach upholstered banquette next to him and dowsed his plate in salt, pepper, Tabasco, and a thick layer of ketchup.

It took Billy fifteen minutes of determined labor to clean his plate. Once done, he left a ten and a five on the table and grabbed the newspaper, carrying it in front of him like a cafeteria tray. Jean caught him on the way out the door.

"Bye, Billy! Don't forget to hit the showers, sweetheart."

She held out a handful of brass tokens for the drivers' showers and pressed the worthless discs into his meaty palm. He looked at the coins and then stuffed them into the pocket of his pants, which already bulged with change, fuel receipts, key rings, his cellphone, and his St. Christopher medal.

"It's not Thursday, Jean."

"No Billy, it's only Monday, but an extra shower never hurt anybody!"

"Yeah. Right. Night, Jean."

The cold bit his cheeks as he opened the door of the coffee shop and stepped out into the fluorescent night. The snow had stopped and the temperature had dropped. The passing storm clouds glowed orange in the city lights as they blew east toward the Palomino Ranch. The few regulars shivering from their trucks to the outbuildings greeted him on his way to his idling truck, which was as warm as he'd left it.

He stripped to his filthy white underpants, put his favorite Patsy Cline album, *Lullabies,* into the overhead CD changer and climbed under a soiled SpongeBob Squarepants comforter in the lower bunk of his sleeper, a small bedroom centered behind the two front captain's chairs in the cab of the Peterbilt. This was home. It was all he needed. He slept on the large mattress, and there was a smaller upper berth that folded flat against the wall above him—although he'd never had any overnight guests. He kept inviting Anise. She had promised they could do it in his sleeper on one of his next visits, but they hadn't yet.

The stock sleeper in a semi is the size of an office cubicle. Billy had started tricking his out and couldn't stop. Tubes of LED lighting snaked around the interior, pulsing from red to blue to green and back in an endless rainbow cycle of light. The walls were quilted velvet with brass nail heads anchoring the fabric. He had a 12-volt microwave, mini refrigerator, and a DVD/TV combo mounted to the sidewall on a swivel bracket where he could watch while lying on his mattress. He'd spent so much on aftermarket parts for his truck that the lawyer overseeing the trust set up by the insurance company had to cap Billy's monthly allowance for home improvements.

He dimmed the tube lights, sang along to his favorite song (he'd been called "crazy" since he was a boy and liked to pretend she sang it just for him) and fell asleep, lulled by the vibration of his idling engine and Patsy's sweet Shenandoah twang.

Billy awoke to the rumble of the trucks on either side of him. The sounds of compressed air and revving horsepower had become his alarm clock. Most drivers set out early after just enough sleeper time (some of it dubiously fabricated, their hours spent driving entered as sleeping or resting, the departure and arrival times changed to mask speeding) to satisfy the required hours should their logbooks be scrutinized at the next truck scale. Billy rarely drove before lunch. He hated to drive hungry, and he never had far to go. Snow was falling again, sticking to the ground. He turned off the engine and put on a flannel barn coat for the cold trudge to the diner.

After his usual midday breakfast, Billy returned to his truck and grabbed his notebook, a pen, and the Billy Club. He tucked the notebook in the breast pocket of his XXXL pearl button western shirt and slipped the leather thong of the tapered wooden club over his right wrist. He began with the tires on his own truck and empty trailer, whacking each one with the club to see if there was any gummy give or telltale thunk of a flat.

Satisfied, he moved through the lot, now enveloped in a knee-deep mist from the melting snow on the warming blacktop. He began checking the tires on the remaining trucks. Anytime he found a flat (or a loose chain binder, ripped tarp, broken light, shifting load, or any other potential trouble for a fellow driver), he wrote a description of the cab, the name of the trucking company and the DOT number of the truck in his notebook and headed into the shop to make his daily report. Billy's routine saved the drivers thousands of dollars every month in "fix-it" tickets, often written at truck scales for burned out lights, loose air lines and misadjusted brakes. He also increased the service profit for the truck shop every month, ensuring that worn tires and other bad parts were replaced at the Outpost and not further west in Sacramento or east in Winnemucca or Salt Lake City. For his efforts, drivers and the shop foreman would often slip Billy a ten, sometimes even a twenty-dollar bill.

Billy had almost worked his way through the half-empty lot when he spotted a truck he hadn't seen before idling at the far end. It was an older Kenworth reefer from Alabama. As he was checking the tires on the driver's side, the door flew open, and a slim man wearing only a scowl, flannel boxer shorts, and a pair of worn cowboy boots jumped off the top of the gas tank. The man glared at Billy.

"What in the hell do you think you're doing?" The driver shouted over the compressor and looked Billy over. "You fucking retard! Get the hell away from my truck." The driver grabbed the end of the Billy Club and yanked. The leather thong dug into Billy's skin, then snapped. The driver raised the smooth black wood high overhead. "If I catch you near my truck again, I'm gonna—"

Billy Donovan was nimble for an obese man, and strong. Before the driver could sidestep his lunge, Billy was on top of him on the wet asphalt, his club back in hand. It only took one blow for Billy to knock the man unconscious.

Billy watched the thin, almost naked driver for a moment. He'd sprawled spread-eagled onto the pavement, coming to rest on his back. The steam rising off the asphalt made him look magic, like he was swimming in clouds. His skinny chest was moving, stretching the skin taut over his visible ribcage.

The thin man's still, square jaw was bristled grey. Satisfied the man would no longer bother him, Billy finished checking the reefer truck and found one of the inner tires was flat. Billy scribbled in his notebook, stepped over the prone driver, and finished checking the three remaining trucks before heading into the shop.

John, the shop foreman, stood behind the service desk.

"Morning, Billy. Give me a second to help this gentleman and I'll go over your report with you," he said, taking paperwork from a driver. Billy sat on a vinyl chair and thumbed through a huge aftermarket parts catalog. When the other driver walked out, he flipped open his notebook and slid the day's dog-eared page of notes across the counter.

There were six flat or low tires in the lot, a load that looked like it had shifted, and a loose tarp on a hay wagon. Billy finished up his report.

"And there's a guy laying on the ground next to his truck and it has a flat too. His truck is a green Kenworth. His truck is from Alabama."

"Did you say he's laying on the ground?"

"Yup."

"Did he look hurt?"

"Not before I hit him."

"You punched a driver?"

"I hit him with the Billy Club."

"Jesus, Billy! Take me to him. Now!"

The driver had come to and was on his hands and knees trying to regain his senses. He shivered in the cold air as Billy and John approached him.

"Get the hell away, you goddamn retard!" he yelled at Billy. When he raised his head to speak he looked like a dog barking.

"Easy, man," John purred in the same voice he used to soothe irate customers at the shop. "Billy—go back to your truck and wait for me there."

"But, but—"

"Billy, go to your truck and wait." John squatted next to the man, who remained on his hands and knees in the snow.

"Okay."

Billy knew he was in trouble for hitting the man with his club. John was mad at him. He worried they might take his truck away and not let him drive anymore. That wasn't fair because he lived in his truck. He wouldn't let anybody take away his house. He climbed into the driver's seat and thought. Several minutes later, he climbed down from the cab and walked to his trailer. He cranked down the landing gear. He unhooked the air lines from the back of the cab. He unlocked the kingpin on the fifth wheel. He gave everything one final look and climbed back into the driver's seat. He started the engine, and as soon as the air pressure built up enough to release his brakes, he pulled the long way out of the lot.

John opened the door of the stupefied driver's Kenworth sleeper and grabbed a comforter, a wool blanket, and a foam rubber pillow shaped like the bottom of an egg carton. The little guy sat cross-legged in the fresh snow and shivered. John could count his ribs through the sun-wrinkled turkey skin of his chest. His forearms were all sinew and tendon encased in scabby, bruised parchment. He had a tattoo of a galloping horse on his shoulder. John laid the comforter on the snowy asphalt and helped the man slide onto it. He swaddled him in the blanket and placed the foam block beneath his head, from which sprouted thick, stringy brown hair that needed a cut. Billy had whacked him good with the club, and the man might have a slight concussion, but besides a swollen left eye and a killer headache, he thought the guy probably wasn't much worse off than when he woke up this morning.

Once the driver was able to get on his feet, he eased himself into his sleeper, tugging on John and the chrome grab bar bolted to the side of his truck. He dressed in blue jeans and a down vest over a green T-shirt with a small yellow trailer on the chest, and set a straw cowboy hat, stained with a dark crown of sweat and hair gel, atop his head.

John led him to the coffee shop, bought him breakfast, and had the waitress bring a batch of ice cubes wrapped in a dingy dishtowel. His name was Fred Pollard, and he held the lumpy frozen mass on his swollen face, leaning into the rag with his eyes closed. Pollard was livid. When he finished with his vulgarity-laced story, John knew he had some leverage—Pollard had raised the club over his head as if to strike Billy, even if he never intended to. In a quiet, calming voice, John laid out his bargain.

By the end of breakfast, Pollard had agreed not to report Billy to the Nevada Highway Patrol. John explained Billy's special status with the regular crowd at the Outpost Truck Stop. They wouldn't take kindly to an outsider getting him locked up or kicked off the road. John pointed out that an altercation between two drivers would guarantee an intense examination of each driver's equipment, log book, driving record, bills of lading, load, sleeper and a DOT drug test. He added that he was one hundred percent sure *Billy's* tests and inspections would come back squeaky clean. The only thing Pollard asked for in return was a couple of free minor repairs in the shop—including the flat tire—and a personal apology from Billy.

Billy loved driving past downtown Reno on the freeway at night. Each building was garishly painted by colored lights shining inward and upward, each casino tower like an onstage performer. It gave the six square blocks a bright rainbow hue enhanced by day-bright entertainment marquees, neon trim, and elaborate architectural facades. This spectacle was beautiful rolling past the driver's window at sixty-five miles an hour.

But in the white glare of an afternoon snowstorm, downtown looked drab. The bleached concrete of unlit casinos through the curtain of ashy flakes made the buildings look like a row of immense bones. Billy rarely ventured into the downtown corridor—the narrow, one-way streets and the haphazard clumps of drunken tourists scared him. His only joy driving downtown was crossing the Truckee River driving north on Lake Street, under the steel framework of the retired Reno Arch, long ago replaced by a bigger, brighter version straddling Virginia Street two blocks to the west.

He preferred the crowd at the truck stop. And the whorehouse. As Billy rolled up the hill out of Reno, he noticed the storm hung thick and dark gray up the Truckee River canyon. The electronic billboard on the Robb Drive overpass did not yet call for chains over the summit, and the inspection station on the Nevada side was still not set up. As long as he got to Donner Summit before the snow piled up on the road, he would not have to pull over and chain up the cab. He made good time up the narrow canyon. Billy sang "Truckin'" out loud whenever he was deadheading. The guys at the Outpost had explained that Deadheads were not the same thing as deadheading—he didn't understand why.

Most guys hated to burn fuel without a paying load behind, but Billy loved to feel the truck speed up the mountain without the tug of a trailer. The swinging pull of towed goods always scared him a little bit, like a growling dog had latched onto the seat of his blue jeans. He rolled his tractor past the batch plant near the Donner Pass Road off ramp and started the steep climb toward the summit. The spitting snow turned to large, uneven flakes that started to stick to the road, obliterating the lane lines as Billy shifted and accelerated up the winding ribbon of truck-worn, weather-pitted concrete.

John could see Billy's empty trailer, askew in its extra-wide spot, from his seat by the coffeehouse window. The snow had picked up in the last half hour, and he decided that Pollard could use another pot of coffee and some Advil before they went out to confront Billy. It was agreed that John would talk to Billy first, then have him apologize to Pollard. Fred was headed westbound and wasn't too keen on chaining up and driving in the snow anyway. He hoped to get started later in the afternoon once the storm had moved on to the east. He'd sped westward from the Dakotas with a load of frozen buffalo meat but had lost time in a series of storms and wouldn't be able to deliver it to Oakland until Monday anyway.

Knowing that his club-wielding adversary was hiding out in his sleeper, Pollard was in no rush to step away from a free meal, and, after a breakfast that could almost rival a Billy Donovan feast, he was enjoying hot black coffee, a piece of fresh Boston Cream pie, and, most of all, the sympathetic attention of Claire, the nineteen-year-old waitress who worked weekday mornings while her mother watched her young daughter. It was another half-hour before John walked alongside Billy's trailer and realized the tractor was not attached.

"What do you mean he's gone?" Fred Pollard was feeling the buzz of his eighth cup of coffee, and the pain reliever was losing its effect.

"Billy's trailer was unhitched and he's bobtailing around somewhere."

"Let's call out the troopers, they'll find him."

"No. There's only two places that he could be headed—one's eastbound, the other west."

"What's westbound?"

"The Blue Canyon exit."

"And east?"

"Palomino Ranch."

"The whorehouse?"

"Yep."

"Then let's head eastbound, friend." Pollard smiled, revealing caffeine- and nicotine-yellowed teeth and a gap where a front incisor had long been missing, "I'm puttin' this one on the retard's tab."

Billy squinted ahead through the blowing snow as he drove past the summit sign and rest area, and conditions didn't improve at all on the downslope. A chain control had gone into effect several miles behind him, and he saw only a few cars traveling west with him on the divided highway. Each passing car startled him. A pair of headlights would emerge out of the blizzard as dull yellow starbursts, then fade red into the storm ahead. As the cars pulled alongside him, he feared he would see flashing lights and hear a loudspeaker ordering him to pull over to be arrested for hurting the mean, skinny little driver. Or killing him. He had to creep along in the slow lane and watch for the guardrails and road markers in order to stay on the road. His hands began to ache from the tension of clutching the wheel. Driving in a Sierra snowstorm required a great deal of concentration—something immensely difficult for Billy. The snow streaking at his windshield reminded him of the Millennium Falcon's jump into hyper drive, which helped him ignore the sick feeling in his belly—the fear of what might happen to him, to his truck, to his life. By the time he reached Blue Canyon, there were a few inches of snow on the road.

Billy pulled off into the extra wide shoulder lane for trucks. About every tenth of a mile stood a porta-potty, and Billy passed three of them until he found the right spot and pulled to the edge of the blacktop. This was where his mom had died.

Just ten feet from the widened shoulder stood a gleaming, white wooden cross with the misspelled name *Jack-ee Donavan* crudely handwritten in black Sharpie. A chrome Jesus was bolted on the front of the cross. Billy had found the Savior in a catalog on the counter of the chrome shop that normally sold skulls, longhorn cattle, and the silhouettes of nude women to trim out mud flaps.

"I don't want the dead Jesus," Billy said when he'd put in the order. "I want him happy with his arms out, like when he parted the ocean."

"I think that was Moses," the man taking his order replied.

"No. It was Jesus." Billy was mad that the man questioned his Bible smarts.

Billy knelt beside the little memorial and stroked the top of the cross. "Hi, Mom. I think I'm in trouble."

He kissed the top of the cross and squatted cross-legged in the snow. After a few minutes, he felt the sting of cold through his insulated coveralls. By then he was dusted in snow and the canvas fabric was stiff with frost.

It was a twenty-minute drive from the Outpost Truck Stop to the Palomino Ranch brothel in good weather. With the slick roads, it took John and Pollard forty-five minutes in the shop's one-ton utility truck. Pollard was dumbfounded that Billy owned his rig outright despite the fact that he rarely had a paying load, usually deadheading Interstate 80 between Reno and Sacramento, picking up the occasional short haul along the way. John told him about Billy's mom's accident, how she had died of a broken neck, her body cradled in the arms of the first person to arrive on scene—a trucker from Stockton who was hauling a shipping container to the Port of

Oakland. When Billy received the proceeds of his mother's life insurance policy and the first payment from a trust she had set up to care for him, he found his used rig for sale at the Peterbilt dealership and wrote a check for the truck he wasn't even licensed to drive. The ongoing monthly checks paid for driver's school, and were more than enough to cover food and diesel—with plenty left over for his love of chrome, lights, horns and other needless accessories. It had taken Billy three years of trucking school and the help of the Outpost regulars before the fat man-child finally had his CDL.

"So why the hell does he drive back and forth over the same road?"

"He likes to head up to the little memorial he built for his mom."

"So why are we coming out here then? Is Billy some kinda pussy hound?"

John smiled. "I guess you could say that. Truth is, he's got himself a girlfriend of sorts here. When something's bothering him he sometimes comes out here to see her."

"Does he pay her? I mean, do they...*fuck*?"

"Of course. Billy may be slow, but he understands business well enough. Besides, she doesn't charge him more than her average rate."

"You're kidding me. She doesn't jack up her prices to sleep with that slobbering fat ass?"

"Easy, Fred. Billy's a friend to a lot of people. Myself included."

"Right," he laughed, "but he did knock the shit out of me. Maybe I'll take *his* girl for a spin."

They parked the truck in the large gravel lot and walked through a small wrought iron gate. John rang the bell and pushed the heavy security door when the buzzer sounded. They walked into a dim room with a bar on one end, a pool table in the center, and several plush couches. A woman in her early sixties greeted them from behind the bar.

"Hey, Johnny! It's nice to have some company. You and your friend want a beer?"

"No thanks, Estelle. Billy been in today?"

"Nope, and I wasn't expecting him. Anise's next shift ain't till next week."

"Alright. Thanks."

"You boys leavin' so soon?"

John looked at Pollard and raised his eyebrows. Pollard smiled and nodded to Estelle. "I think we better wait out this weather before we get back on the road."

"I guess I'll take that beer then, Estelle." John walked over to the bar. Pollard would be at least an hour.

Billy knew the road was slippery and white in either direction, and he didn't want to get in more trouble for not having chains on when he was supposed to. He had a microwave lasagna in his little fridge and a stack of his favorite DVDs. He decided to spend the night in the truck parking area and hope for the storm to end by morning, so he could turn around and head back to the Outpost. He felt better after talking to his mom, but he knew he was still in trouble for thunking the man's head. But the little man had started screaming "retard" at him and tried to hit him with *his* own club.

He left the engine idling to power the heater and microwave. He zapped his dinner before stripping to his skivvies and climbing under his SpongeBob blanket. He put Patsy Cline on the stereo and pulled a small paper bag from under the mattress of his sleeper bed. This was a frequent evening routine. In the bag was a stack of eight Polaroid photos that Anise had her friend Cheyenne take. His number one girl had posed just for Billy, and each shot got raunchier. The first showed the oval-faced black girl in lacy red lingerie, and in the final shot she posed naked in Billy's favorite position, on all fours, her face turned, smiling over her shoulder. Anise told him she liked to do it that way best because then Billy didn't squish her like he did when he was on top. She called it *doggy*, which made him laugh. He ended up liking it because it made him come faster than any other way.

Billy pulled out his photos and put them on top of his mattress. He pulled his underpants off and stuffed them onto a small shelf above the bed. He looked back and forth at the different snapshots and worked himself off, lying face down to minimize the mess. Once he'd finished, he was very sleepy. He smiled at the smooth brown body posing naked on the comforter next to him. He liked sleeping here at the parking area, but he always felt sleepy and a little guilty after a fit of masturbation; it made him feel like his mom was sleeping in the room next door, just like when she was alive.

Fred Pollard was a little more flush than John had thought, and they didn't leave the Palomino until almost two hours later. By then, John had downed several beers at the bar and had lost $25 to Estelle on the pool table. The snow hadn't let up, and John decided they should head back to the Outpost to let Pollard catch some sleeper time, then head up to Blue Canyon in the morning to find Billy. If they rode up tomorrow morning in Fred's rig, he'd be halfway to Sacramento by eight o'clock. John could hitch a ride back with Billy.

John dropped Pollard off at his truck and headed to the shop. By the time John finished his paperwork and headed home to sleep, Pollard was already pulling his truck out of the tire shop and back out into the lot to do the same.

The two men met for an early breakfast in the coffee shop and merged onto I-80 westbound at about six-thirty. The road had been sanded, salted and plowed to the pavement after having been closed for several hours during the night. They made good time and Pollard appreciated having John along, not only for company, but because he also knew the curves and long climbs and relentless downgrades of this stretch of road. They reached the Blue Canyon parking area a little after nine. Billy's truck was covered in a foot of snow and parked right where John had said it would be. A moonscape of wind-drifted snow obscured the truck's hard lines and the wheels had disappeared in serried mounds.

John knocked on the sleeper door of the shining purple tractor.

"Billy. Billy, it's John. Wake up, buddy!" John knocked several more times on Billy's sleeper, then looked back at Pollard's idling truck and shrugged. After a few minutes, John opened the unlocked driver's door.

A thick atmosphere of warmth, the sweet voice of Patsy Cline, and the mingled scents of lasagna and sour body odor enveloped the cab. Snow had drifted against the vertical windshield and everything was cocooned in a dull grey-white glow. The curtain behind the seats separating the sleeper from the cab was closed, and John called Billy's name once before pulling the heavy blue velour aside. Billy lay face down, covering the entire mattress with his naked girth, the absurd pink body sprawled across the sleeper. Mounds of fatty tissue gave way to gullies and foothills of rolled skin. The crack of Billy's ass sprouted tufts of wiry hair, and his cheeks looked like a set of pimpled mud flaps. One arm rested under his torso, and the other clutched two glossy pictures of Anise. A pile of several other photos was on the mattress nearby, resting on a brown paper bag. John patted the massive shoulders and noticed that they were cold despite the stifling heat of the sleeper.

"Billy?" It took John a moment to realize that Billy was not asleep. "Billy. Billy! Wake up, goddammit!" John looked at the massive naked body splayed in front of him. Underneath the corpulence something had burst. A vessel or an artery. Or the overworked heart had simply stopped.

He took the photos from Billy's hand. He placed the stack back in the paper bag and pulled the SpongeBob blanket over Billy's head.

Pollard waited with John until the Highway Patrol arrived.

"Sorry about old Billy," he said.

"Yup. It's too damn bad. It's a goddamn bad thing…he would've apologized, you know."

"Yeah. I feel bad about what happened."

John could not think of anything to say to fill the long awkward pause. Finally, Pollard mumbled, "Well, see ya around, John."

John watched the Kenworth disappear down the road and returned to answering the patrolman's questions. An hour later, the lawyers had been called and the coroner arrived to pick up the body. John signed off as next of kin so he could take charge of Billy when they were done with him. The coroner performed an autopsy because the death was "unattended," and John was not surprised when the results revealed a heart attack brought on by obesity, untreated diabetes, and clogged arteries.

Many of the Outpost regulars pitched together with John, lobbying the state to put in a small, permanent rest area where the truck parking lane and porta-potties still stand, but no one seemed to be able to get the right approvals or find the money in the budget.

Instead, set back from the side of the road at the edge of an old growth pine forest cascading up to the tree line of the granite peaks above, two large steel crosses stand in place of Jackie's old wooden one. From the front of each cross, an un-crucified Jesus blesses the westbound traffic, arms outstretched in gleaming chrome.

STEEP

The sky was a mute blue. The rising sun had gained the edge of the peaks across the valley and was painting the crystals of new-fallen snow with bursts of umber fire and yellow starbursts. As the great orb rose, the blue deepened and electrified—an unreal postcard shade that mirrored cerulean shoals of the great lake behind him. As the heat rose from the desert below, the crystals lost their shape and began to cohere. And he knew, far below, people were lining up for the chairlifts and heading his way, seeking their own fresh tracks.

Doug Pearson's breath hung in his throat. As he peered over the edge, vertigo began to take hold—stirring his gut and clenching his sphincter. Anything less than total commitment was guaranteed to cause massive pain, if not death.

Below the edge of the cornice on which he perched, the world fell away, invisible for thirty feet until the fifty-degree slope came into view. Two hundred feet down the fall line he could see the serrated black of exposed rocks that marked two cliff bands. The first was a mandatory huck off a natural cornice to plunge for twenty vertical feet. The second offered the option of a shoulder-wide chute bisecting it on skier's left. The new snow and over-the-ridge winds of last night's storm had loaded the upper slope, and he knew that once he hit the funnel below the rocks, he would have to burn speed and turn hard to let his slough go by or risk getting swallowed up in the sliding white wave of his own making.

He fidgeted with his poles, reached up to adjust his goggles, and sighed, raising a beastlike head of steam that coated his lenses with a thin layer of ice. Knowing that overthinking is as bad as not planning, he coiled the twin springs of his legs and leaped up and outward, relishing the air beneath his skis.

Herbert Weiss, Tamarack's "Old Man of the Mountain," raised a small metal flask high above his head, nodding to Doug and the rest of the gathered tribe. A decade after Doug's reputation-making run, known forever as "Pearson's Plunge," he and his compatriots still managed to be on the mountain nearly every day.

"Prost!" the Austrian called. The guttural high-alpine Deutsch lodged in the recesses of his throat. He pressed the metal neck of the flask to his lips and emptied it in a series of gulps.

"Prost!" responded the handful of skiers and boarders huddled in the bunker, sipping from cans of Pabst Blue Ribbon and Battle Born Beer left to chill all day in the snow. This weekly ritual had once been one of the highlights of Doug's life. It was right up there with learning five months ago that Meagan was pregnant with their first child.

Lately, though, the revelation of his upcoming paternity had been weighing on Doug. He was teary-eyed when he heard the news. He thought of teaching a child to ski, traveling the world as a family, raising a child to enjoy the beauty and exhilaration of the natural world. But soon, Meagan was after him about how much time he spent away from the house. Their sex life became a struggle. His wife was moody and didn't want to be touched half the time. Her breasts were getting bigger, changing shape; the nipples became dark puffy targets of his lust, but she didn't want his hands or mouth on them. The rising loaf of her belly had become more than just a physical impediment between them in the bed. As she flipped and twisted next to him, he dreamed he was trapped in her uterus, the skin of her belly stretching to keep him forever contained.

Doug felt his buzz sliding away as he thought of his wife moping around their house, but with impeccable timing, the joint made its way back to him. He took a long, slow toke. He felt the magic smoke warm him inside as the frigid wind bit at his cheeks through the unglazed windows of the bunker.

Doug was among nine other derelict snow bums sprawled in varying states of bliss inside the log and dirt structure hidden in the wild backside terrain Tamarack Ridge was famous for.

Today had a feeling of final celebration. All those gathered knew they were up against a grave inevitability. The small, day-tripper mountain, frequented by locals, had been on an unpublicized mission of upgrading chairlifts, bathrooms, and the locker room. Bourgeois menu items began moving out of the cafeteria kitchen—sushi rolls, egg-drop soup, hot artichoke and parmesan appetizers. When the small ski hills without overnight facilities began catering to out-of-town ski-trippers, a corporate purchase of one of the last great hometown resorts was certain. Massive development would follow soon after.

The smell of the pot, the smoky sausages roasting on the bunker's little grill, and the sharp aroma of the surrounding pines satiated Doug. He sighed and let his worries ebb out with his canned-beer-scented breath. It had been weeks since Doug spent a Friday morning skiing, and a hell of a long time since he'd done it drunk and stoned. He no longer felt his own weight on the hard dirt floor of the bunker. His body seemed to stay suspended an inch or two above, a tingle radiating from his head and chest out to the ends of his limbs. This makeshift bunker had been his second home for going on ten years, ever since that one glorious run had earned him cachet with the local ski bums and hardcore rippers drawn to the rough couloirs and backwoods of the mountain. The unofficial proprietor of the bunker was Herbert Weiss, who'd never lost his thick Tyrolean accent, despite thirty years on the shores of Lake Tahoe. He was part of the mountain at Tamarack.

"Doug, why don't you just quit your *Scheisse* warehouse job and patrol up here full time?" asked Weiss, whose red turtleneck bulged at the belly, overhanging the waistband of his powder pants. Doug could never tell if the Austrian's face was red with sunburn or inebriation; it had been the same ruddy shade since he had first known the old man. As Weiss laughed, Doug was struck with a pungent wave of fermented pears—the scent of Obstler, Weiss's homemade brandy.

"I wish I had the balls to, Herby." A breeze, chilled by its trip across the gunmetal grey lake to the west, pushed the blue smoke across his face. Doug dabbed his stinging eyes and smiled at Weiss.

Tamarack's new Resort Operations General Manager walked through the day lodge. He attempted to blend in with the midweek ski crowd by foregoing his hand-tailored suit and sterling snowflake cufflinks for a pair of khaki slacks and a button-down shirt with a navy overcoat. On the left lapel was a pewter nametag: *Albert Blander.* A plaid cashmere scarf swathed his thin white neck, another conscious effort at casual sophistication. Clipboard in hand, he wound his way through the ski-booted, puffy-pantsed crowd queuing up for nine-dollar cheeseburgers and quick-bite snacks. Blander kept halting in the middle of heavily trafficked areas, forcing people to cut hard around him while he took copious notes before moving on with a smug smile on his otherwise expressionless face.

He knew this ramshackle, plywood and corrugated metal lodge would soon be a relic in the collective memory of the working class day skiers who congregated here. Its replacement, after a few thin "growing" seasons spent breaking ground, cutting trees, and waiting out the recession, would rival any riverstone and timber palace in Aspen, Whistler, or even the Alps. The carpenters, cocktail waitresses, and delivery drivers who could still afford the $400 season passes would be replaced by the moneyed tenants of the partial-ownership condos and custom homes. For all his trouble, Blander would become the czar of his own mountain kingdom, complete with onsite residence, a corporate ski pass, and access to the company jet. He kicked his fleece-lined Italian loafer at a filthy black spot on the worn indoor-outdoor carpet and made a note in his folder: *seal slate floor with industrial-grade finish.*

When ski patroller Wallace Jensen dropped into the log bunker, Herby Weiss greeted the hulking figure and offered him a shot of pear brandy that Jensen declined with a smile and gloved palm.

"Thanks, Herby. I'm working."

"Howdy, Wally." Doug switched the joint to his left hand, extending his right toward the patroller, who, with a warm smile, removed his gloves to shake Doug's hand.

Jensen sighed. "Guys," he slapped his gloves on his thigh and glanced at the floor of the bunker, "it's happening."

At his dawn shift, he'd noticed the batteries in his radio were dying and had gone to the supply closet to replace them. As he passed the Special Tickets office, he saw that the door to the small lunch room behind it was open. What Jensen discovered there meant their years of collective dread had finally been realized.

Blander finished his rounds of the day lodge and returned to his new basement office just behind the Special Tickets counter. He had been warned that his presence might cause a panic among the employees; his superiors asked him to maintain a low profile and keep his office door locked at all times. He passed the counter without acknowledging the two women behind it and slid into his office, closing and locking the door behind him. He rested his hands on a huge Plexiglas case set on a waist-high table, and squinted at the tiny buildings inside. He had already picked out his condo—a third floor penthouse with a view of the Mount Rose summit to the east. The phone on his desk rang, and he wiped his fingerprints from the case with his shirt cuff before answering.

Larry "Freeheel" Franks pried open the door of Blander's office with an edge file and entered at the head of the pack, which included Doug, Weiss, longtime Tamarack local Ed "Snowshoe" Thompson, and Luisa Agra, an Argentine who came to Tamarack Ridge as a liftie three years ago on a winter work visa and never went home. Freeheel waited until they all piled into the small space and Luisa closed the door before turning on the light in the windowless room. Against the wall facing the door stood a small desk with a multi-line telephone, a fax machine, and a three-drawer file cabinet. Weiss pressed his face against a Plexiglas box, which held a scale model of Tamarack Ridge, set up on the large table where the staff used to drink coffee and eat lunch. This would be where prospective buyers would select their condos and lots when this office (and the Special Tickets counter) opened as the Tamarack Mountain Spa and Snowsports Resort Sales Office in one week. With the exception of the existing chairlifts, represented by thin wires, the miniature resort was almost unrecognizable with its sprawling complex of buildings, plazas, and paved arteries.

The day parking lot had disappeared, and in its place sprouted a facsimile of a large pedestrian village complete with shops, restaurants, and three stories of condominiums above the storefronts. Roads and cul de sacs crisscrossed the mountain's base, and custom home sites crammed into the trees and onto the existing runs. A hotel filled the area where the ski school now congregated. A painted red line ran downhill and off the edge of the table. Red tendrils branched off the line, running to each complex of buildings and homes. Stuck in the center of the line, a small flag read, "Underground Utility Project—Phase One (completed—Fall)." Weiss studied the red artery where it vanished at the edge of the model, the simulated mountain cut away at a sheer cliff, flush with the edge of the Plexiglas.

Six days later, Freeheel, Luisa, Ed Thompson, and Doug met Weiss in the bunker just before the lifts closed. In less than a week, the crew had brainstormed riotous acts of vandalism, overt protests, and underhanded methods of resistance to the corporate takeover. In a substance-addled decision of collective inspiration, the group swore to engage in the most destructive and effective deterrent they could think of. After plotting fires (too hard to contain), chairlift and grooming equipment sabotage (they didn't want to deprive themselves of ski days), and the ill-advised suggestion of kidnapping Albert Blander, they decided to disable the new sewer line. Tamarack had always been on a septic system that limited the number of daily users. By installing the sewer line, the new owners gave the mountain an unlimited capacity to shit and piss the locals' dreams of a small day resort down the mountain.

Doug kept looking at Weiss's backpack resting on the frozen dirt floor. It contained enough high explosives to destroy the bunker and shred everyone in it to strips of skin and synthetic fabric tatters. Freeheel pulled a smoldering joint from somewhere in his tangled grey beard and passed it around the circle. They all shared a thermos of hot coffee and a cluster of hot bratwursts that Weiss had wrapped in foil. As the sun slipped behind Tamarack Peak, the temperature in the bunker tumbled ten degrees in twenty minutes. The group huddled and talked to pass the time. Sometime after 6:30 they decided that Ski Patrol had completed its customary sweep, looking for lost skiers and misplaced gloves, poles and goggles, and they could ski down undetected.

Everyone had done their best to wear black from head to toe. Weiss had the hardest time with this. The best he could muster was a navy blue knit sweater dotted with bright white snowflakes. There were other slips of camouflage etiquette: Luisa Agra donned a fuzzy pink headband to keep her ears warm. Larry Franks wore a checked flannel shirt and a hunter's cap with a sheepskin lining. Most of the backpacks stuffed with supplies had reflective tape or shiny patches of plastic that picked up even the slightest light. These had been covered over with black electrical tape. The group had been smart enough to pick the night of a new moon, so there was little chance anyone would notice them in the semi-dark forest—as long as they stayed well away from the highway.

The little troop of mountain guerillas emerged from the bunker and Weiss, using a series of complicated hand signals, attempted to align them for their assault. Finally, he gave up and briefed them, reminding them of their timed departures and various rendezvous points.

"Five minute intervals. Meet below the parking lot and regroup."

Freehill clipped into his skis first, locking just the toes of his boots into his namesake Telemark bindings. The others gathered into their gear, fanned out, and began their descent.

With no light to reveal the drops, bumps, and rapid changes in terrain, Doug was almost tossed off his feet several times. He steered for the yellow-blue vibration of the mercury vapor security light on the back of the day lodge and found his way to the parking lot from memory, arriving first. He wedged himself against a wall of snow plowed by one of the resort's giant, ancient loaders and, like a child about to start trouble, laughed.

"Okay, let's go over the plan one more time." Weiss used his Teutonic accent and unmistakable clipped military tone to his full advantage. The oversized knit snowflakes on his sweater looked, in the low light, like campaign ribbons and garish medals of valor. He was hauling all the explosives, so it was his mission to lead. "Freeheel and Snowshoe, you will lead us through the trees and find us the best line to ski down to our first point. Doug, you partner with Luisa and make sure that the group isn't spotted. I will stay a good distance from all of you, just to be safe. Keep five minutes between each group. I'll see you there."

Doug was anxious. Luisa's English was very good, but he still found communication with her awkward. He first saw her three seasons ago, loading skiers on the summit chair while he stood in the lift line. Most lifties were androgynous robots in matching powder-blue ski jackets, but she had curves, even in her unisex, all-weather work uniform. It had been a windy day, and even with her hood and goggles obscuring her face, Doug found her attractive in some unconventional way that he couldn't quite name. The goggles rested on a long nose that plumped at the end. A small diamond stud punctuated the left nostril. She smiled at him through thin, chapped lips. Her eye teeth were more prominent than their neighbors, giving her a fanged, canine smile. Behind the amber lenses, Doug could see her large brown eyes. While skating through the empty line to board the lift, Doug stared one moment too long and hooked his ski tip on a post holding up the queue ropes. He twisted around backwards and fell hard. Luisa helped him up, pulling his entire weight up with just one arm. They met through mutual friends later that day in the lodge and developed a pleasant acquaintance punctuated by flirtatious teasing. Ever since their first encounter, she made sure his embarrassment was long-lived—every time he boarded a chair she was working, she would hit a button, slowing it to the lethargic crawl used to load small children.

Snowshoe and Freeheel exhaled steaming clouds of hot breath. They shouldered their packs and skis and crouched behind the high wall of snow on the shoulder of the highway. Making sure there was no traffic headed their way, they walked as fast as their stiff boots would allow across both lanes of icy blacktop and into the trees on the other side. Five minutes later, Weiss did the same. After five more minutes, Doug was about to break away when Luisa grabbed him by the sleeve of his ski jacket. She nodded toward the road. Headed up the road was a single set of headlights.

Albert Blander hated driving the highway after dark. The black ice and hairpin turns made him grip the wheel so that his hands tingled by the time he pulled into the Tamarack parking lot. Every Friday night, Blander had to drive back up to his mountainside office to check in with United Ski Corporation headquarters in France. He gave a weekly progress update on his resort analysis and uploaded any pertinent information on the development and human resources aspects of USKI's largest North American project to date.

He pulled his silver SUV into the parking lot and down the pedestrian walkway, parking in front of the main entrance to the day lodge. From there it was a quick walk down the stairs and into his little office behind the Special Tickets counter. He had an hour before he needed to call France. He pulled the blanket from the display case and admired the mini resort. He fondled the edge of the Plexiglas and imagined himself standing in front of the village and cutting a ribbon with a giant pair of scissors.

Eight hundred feet below the lodge's parking area, out of sight of the road, Freeheel Franks and Ed Thompson cut tracks through the ponderosa pines, doing their best to stay in the treeless swath of the utility corridor running downhill toward the next curve of the highway. They reached the edge of the road, removed their skis and crossed, disappearing into the woods. Weiss arrived five minutes behind them and clomped across the empty highway. The weight of his pack caused cramps in his back and legs, and he wasn't sure how much longer he would be able to ski upright. Still, tonight was their best chance and he didn't want to be the reason they didn't go through with their mission. He knew that he'd never talk them into it again.

Huddled in the trees a few hundred feet above the others, Doug and Luisa waited.

"Cold," Luisa smiled, hooking her arm around Doug's and nuzzling her head against his. He wasn't sure what to make of her sudden proximity. "Exciting night, don't you think?"

Doug had started the evening in a great mood, but fear and paranoia had set in. Now Luisa was adding a whole new element. Having her here, and as his vandal buddy, complicated the already stressful situation. Not only might they get arrested, but now he felt guilty, lying to his pregnant wife about where he was, sure that every set of headlights coming up the highway was a Washoe County Sheriff's Department four-wheel-drive.

"We've got to get moving in two minutes—"

Luisa cut him off, covering his mouth with her parted lips. She rolled him onto his back and pawed at his jacket, grinding her hips against the front of his powder pants. He couldn't decide whether or not he should push her off—the twin grips of desire and guilt locked him in indecisiveness.

She pulled off her mittens and unzipped her parka. She began to pull her sweater over her head, revealing a lacy black bra, which Doug thought she filled admirably. The high beams of an approaching car lit the pine trees above her head.

"Doug!" she complained as he pushed her off—and a good way down the hill, where she collapsed in a pile of snow.

"Stay down!" The car passed, and Doug watched the taillights to make sure that the driver hadn't tapped the brakes. "It's time!" he said. "Let's go."

She zipped up, and Doug laid out both pairs of skis for them to click in and continue on to the next rendezvous with the crew.

The entire group reformed twenty minutes past the planned time. Doug knew he was safe from Luisa in the company of the three other men, but he disliked the carpool arrangements— he was supposed to drive her back to her rented house in town. That was the least of his worries now. It occurred to Doug that, on top of feeling up another woman in the dark woods while his pregnant wife waited at home thinking he was at a Volunteer Patrol meeting, blowing up private property with high explosives could cost him much more than a divorce. But Weiss was a persuasive bastard, and Doug saw no way to back out now. Besides, this was his chance to add to his legacy. A chance to re-up his yellowing credentials with the ski bums and the locals. He wasn't going to stand by and watch as one of the last great ski mountains in the country became another corporate-designed village with high-rise condos and cloned retail boutiques.

Weiss led them to the edge of a steep ridge that dropped almost one hundred feet to the highway below. A mile below that, Doug could see the haphazard, grounded constellation of yellow lights in Sierra Pines Estates out in the sagebrush below the tree line. He tried to figure out which one was his house.

The protruding metal elbow of the underground utility sleeve was right where the map said it would be. Here the massive pipe emerged from the underground trench that had been dug from Tamarack's base area, and turned almost ninety degrees back into the ground at the edge of the cliff. This had been one of the trickiest sections to build—Doug remembered hearing how the encased sewer pipe and the phone, cable, and power conduit dropped at a sharp angle underground, following the steep contour of the mountain. The sewer pipe had to be widened where this section leveled off to compensate for the increased pressure caused by the sheer force of gravity. This was the only place they could access the closed system without having to dig with trenching equipment.

"Is everybody ready?" Weiss was uncharacteristically serious.

The five of them exchanged looks, nodding.

"Okay then. Ed?"

Ed Thompson pulled a huge socket wrench from his backpack and went to work on the twenty-two bolts holding together the two halves of the elbow. After a few minutes, Freeheel spelled him on the wrench, followed by Doug, Louisa, and Weiss. Thirty-eight minutes later, there was a one-foot gap between two sections of pipe. Inside they could see the conduit that held telephone, electric, and fiber optic cables and the huge insulated pipe of the main sewer line.

Weiss asked the four other mountain guerillas to move up

the ridge and take cover behind a line of granite boulders. Once they were ensconced in their makeshift bomb shelter, he took off his gloves and began to unload the pack, pinching the small cord on the zipper between thumb and forefinger, allowing the tiny symmetrical teeth to slowly work their way apart. He pulled the seven three-inch by eight-inch explosive hand charges out and arranged them in a small, neat circle. From a separate compartment, he removed seven lengths of pre-measured detonating cord and began to wrap each of the hand charges with a length of fuse.

Doug felt Louisa's breath on the back of his neck as they huddled fifty feet above Weiss. No one spoke as they watched him take the blasting caps from the bag and crimp them to the end of each stick with a special pair of pliers hanging from a lanyard attached to his jacket. This was the same method the Tamarack Ridge Ski Patrol used to run their avalanche control routes every morning. Wallace Jensen had catalogued the seven missing charges as duds in the patrol logbook.

Finally, Weiss removed an igniter from its protective casing and used it to light the first fuse, the longest of the bunch.

"Fire in the hole!" he yelled, and dropped it into the gap in the pipe. The sixty-seven seconds it took for the sound of the explosion to reach them was uneventful except for the bite marks Luisa left on the back of Doug's neck. Weiss lit three more in quick succession and dropped them in the hole. The precisely timed fuses had been trimmed shorter on each successive charge and the explosions were closer to them each time. Porch lights flashed on in the trees far below, and the sound of dogs barking floated up the hill.

Albert Blander sat at his desk bending toward the speaker of his phone, updating his corporate bosses in France, when the phone, lights, computer, and portable heater went out. Seconds later, the echoes of three explosions rolled up the mountain. He leapt from his desk and ran for the door, misjudging the portal by about three feet to the left. He collided hard with a sharp edge and fell to the floor. He heard the display table fall next to him in the dark. Miniature condos jabbed him as he crawled across the floor. The steeple roof of the village clock tower stabbed his knee as he made his way into the Special Ticket Office and toward the exit.

Weiss wrapped the last three charges together with detonation cord. He crimped on the cap, lit the fuse, and dropped the bomb into the gap.

Nothing.

One minute went by, then two. After four minutes had passed, Freeheel yelled down to Weiss, who stood expectantly next to the pipe.

"How long was that fuse, Weiss?"

"Ninety seconds."

"Dud?"

"I think it must—"

A flash of light, a sledgehammer of compressed air from the shock wave, and the burnt smell of explosives swallowed Weiss's voice. The concussion of the blast hit the huddled skiers as they lay prone on the ridge. Bits of metal shrapnel from the pipe, clods of dirt and granite and pine bark rained down on Doug's back. For a moment he couldn't move. After several seconds he managed to find his breath and get to his feet. He ran down to where Weiss had been standing and saw only the ragged ends of the pipe elbow.

"Weiss! Weiss?"

Doug heard movement in the space behind him.

"Boom!" Weiss hooted. "We got the bastards!"

Freeheel and Doug ran over to the Austrian, who was sprawled on his back in the middle of a manzanita bush.

"Can you stand, Herby?"

"I think so."

With Doug grabbing his arm on one side and Freeheel on the other, Weiss rose to his knees. There was a lump of something stuck to Weiss's cheek. Doug tried to wipe it away with his glove, and the white ball swung back to center like a clock pendulum.

"Don't touch my eye please, Doug," Weiss pleaded.

"Oh shit!" Doug's hand flew from the Austrian's face. "We've got to get him to a hospital!" Doug was frantic. "Ski down to the campground and bring up my Suburban. We'll throw him in the back and take him to the emergency room!"

Weiss grabbed Doug's forearm in protest. "You take me to the emergency room, and they'll figure out who was up here bombing the pipe. Take me home—I'll get a ride out of town tomorrow to get my eye fixed."

"Guys?" Snowshoe stood on the edge of the ridge, staring down toward the highway.

"What?" Doug barked, annoyed. He had to think.

"We have to get the hell out of here. We shut down the damn highway."

Freeheel held onto Weiss while Doug and Luisa made their way to the edge of the ridge. One hundred feet below, tons of granite boulders, dirt, trees, snow, and blast debris covered the highway. Once emergency vehicles reached this point, they would investigate the area above the slide. Right where they were standing. Doug figured they had ten, maybe fifteen minutes before emergency crews made it to the debris field. Add another twenty for the sheriff's deputies to make it up to here from the Tahoe side of the mountain, and the ridge would be crawling with cops within the hour.

"We need to gather up all of our gear and ski down to the cars." Ed Thompson had guided in the Sierra for half his life. He'd dug friends' bodies out of avalanches and lost three toes to frostbite. He could run a rescue in any perilous situation without even raising his pulse—though he'd never triaged while trying to avoid arrest. "Take this," he pulled a clean bandana from his pack, "and fill it with ice."

Doug did as he was instructed. Thompson made a snug little blanket for Weiss's eye, folding the cloth gently around it and securing it to the Austrian's cheekbone with Luisa's fleece headband.

"Begin sweeping an area from the rocks," Thompson pointed to their rough bunker above, "to the tree line down there. Don't leave any gloves, hats, wrappers, or boot prints. We have three minutes. Go."

The group covered the area with pine boughs and hunted for any tiny piece of detritus that would incriminate them, before stepping into their skis. Weiss insisted they leave some sort of calling card lest anyone think this was a random prank. He pulled a thick permanent marker from his pocket and wrote *SAVE TAMARACK* in giant block letters on the twisted end of the metal pipe. Then, thinking for a moment, he smiled, pointed to the distended eyeball lashed to his cheek with Luisa's pink headband, and signed, *The Sky Pirates*.

Leading a half-blind Austrian through a dark forest while staying clear of the spotlights on the sheriff's cars was the most extreme bit of skiing any of them had ever done. They'd parked at a summer campground one drainage over from Tamarack's slopes. The county used it as a public sledding hill in the winter, and the parking area was plowed. Doug was excused from driving Luisa home, since she had to take Weiss's car to her house. Doug would drive the Austrian home. After the rest of the group left, Doug insisted on taking Weiss to the ER, but the wounded old man would not allow it.

"You think they won't want to know how my eye came out of its socket while I was dressed in ski gear in the middle of the night? No, we go to my house."

When Doug arrived at his own home, daylight was bathing the summit of Mount Rose in a brilliant pink corona, its peak hiding Tamarack beyond it to the west. Behind the summit, a murky grey wall of cloud warned of a storm rolling in. Meagan was still asleep as he crept into bed.

Doug and the rest of the group were to meet back at the bunker the following day: their typical Saturday routine. After three hours of sleep Doug fumbled down the hallway to the kitchen and started the coffee pot. Meagan was already up watching the news. She was on the brown leather couch, her feet on the matching ottoman, clutching a full-length body pillow to her chest. The dark furniture stood starkly against the white shag carpet she'd picked for the living room with no consideration for the impending mess that would no doubt come with their expected child.

"How was your meeting last night?"

"It ran long. The usual bitching about dues, continuing education requirements, that sort of thing."

"Well, at least you'll be able to stay around here today and help me with the baby's room. Tamarack is shut down."

"What?" The entire mountain?

"Some wacko environmentalists blew up all the utilities and shut down the highway with a giant rockslide. The mountain is closed until Homeland Security and the FBI arrive."

"FBI?

"They think it was orchestrated by an organized group, so the Department of Homeland Security has jurisdiction."

"Oh."

Doug nearly vomited on his couch. What the hell had they done? He'd gone to bed a folk hero and woken up a terrorist. He needed to get together with the other fugitives.

A smooth male voice came from the television, "...they call themselves the 'Sky Pirates,' and authorities say that while it is not a known eco-terrorism group, they are investigating possible ties to the Earth Liberation Front, who burned a ski lodge to the ground in Colorado last summer..."

Jeremy Stevens stood in his Channel 6 fleece jacket at the edge of the rockslide on the highway. Behind him was every local news producer's dream backdrop: three black Suburbans with tinted windows and red and blue lights embedded in the windshields, two helicopters circling above, and an alphabet of blue windbreakers parading past the camera—ATF, FBI, OSHA, DHS, and FEMA.

Weiss would be on his way to Sacramento by now to see if he could save his eye. Doug wondered how he could have slept with the ball dangling on his cheek. He wondered if Weiss's morning stubble irritated it like a hundred wayward eyelashes. Freeheel and Snowshoe were already halfway to the Canadian backcountry by now, and Luisa...well, Doug would have to sort that one out over time. He walked into the kitchen and poured himself a cup of coffee, then sat at the breakfast nook and stared at the vertical lines of his back fence. While he'd been away yesterday, Meagan had begun rearranging the spare bedroom, getting it ready for the baby. On a bench made of old skis were four large cardboard boxes full of Doug's ski posters, old Tamarack banners from the lodge, and, sticking out of the top of the largest box, his ski-boot-shaped water bong. Seeing his favorite things emptied from his only domestic sanctuary gave him a headache, and he felt bile eating away at his esophagus. The doorbell interrupted his fretting.

Doug pictured the group of men clustered on his front porch—sheriff's deputies, FBI men, Feds in dark suits and sunglasses waiting to haul him off in a caravan of armored black SUVs. He thought about slipping out his sliding glass door and vaulting the fence into his neighbor's yard, but an early morning foot chase held no appeal. As he sat pondering his incarceration, Meagan opened the door on a more pressing problem.

"Doug. There's a *Loo-eesa* here to see you."

He walked into the living room and found the women facing each other, Meagan on one side of the doorframe and Luisa, a darkened, distorted funhouse mirror image of his wife on the other. Neither moved. Cool air rushed in through the open doorway, blowing a strand of hair across Meagan's face. She didn't flinch.

"Is there a reason you came by this early?" Meagan crossed her arms over her bulging abdomen and stared down at the tiny Argentine standing on her porch.

Luisa was reduced to a stuttering *"Lo siento"* and a whispered attempt at explanation.

"Come in, Luisa." Doug spoke over his wife's shoulder. Meagan turned to face him, narrowing her eyes. Luisa crept across the threshold and into the living room.

Doug waved Luisa over to the couch. "You must've heard about that thing up at Tamarack. Crazy."

Luisa removed her lambskin-lined boots and dragged her bare toes through the long white strands of the rug. She sat where Doug directed her, lifting the still-warm body pillow and resting it over the arm furthest from her as she perched on the edge of a cushion. He remained standing on the entry hall tile, a half step higher than the living room.

Meagan seated herself in a high-backed leather chair facing the couch and Luisa, taking her time to settle her pregnant body.

In Doug's life, everything was expanding: his relationships, his wife, his ski resort. Each moved outward from the center in deep tremors of complications and dread.

"This is my wife Meagan."

"Hello, Meagan." Luisa smiled, turning her eyes to the white expanse of the living room floor. "I'm sorry to bother you both at home. I came to see if Doug had heard about the… explosion."

"We're in the phone book," Meagan said.

"Yes. I didn't look."

"How did you know where we lived?"

Fuck. Doug had told Luisa they lived in Sierra Pines as they'd huddled together on the mountain, looking out over the vista of lights far below them the night before. He might've even mentioned Jackpine Court. But he'd never given her his street address. He looked across the living room and met Meagan's eyes, which were locked on his face. Over her shoulder he could see his black crew cab pickup truck with oversized tires, its camper shell pocked with ski stickers. Luisa must have driven around until she found his truck.

Once again, the urge to creep out the sliding glass door and vault into the neighbor's yard overtook him. There was a pause as he imagined himself running through yards, out of town, and up the snow-covered mountain, seeking shelter in the bunker perched on the ridge high above. He saw the two women—his wife looking from him to Luisa, Luisa still staring at the shag carpet. He imagined them perched on granite boulders emerging from a vast, white, windblown snowfield. If only they were on the mountain, he'd know what to do.

"I saw the news this morning. Did you try calling Tamarack's main number?"

"There's no answer." Luisa looked at Doug when she spoke. Meagan's pregnant presence cast a shadow on the conversation.

"Maybe you should have driven there first," Meagan stroked the top of her distended belly and smiled at Luisa, "instead of coming to find my husband."

"*Lo siento*. I'm sorry. The road is closed…"

Doug yawned, an old tic when his nerves got the better of him. Meagan marked it from her seat.

"I'll call you if I hear anything." Doug grasped the front door handle and hoped that Luisa would follow his lead. She hopped to her feet. "Thanks for coming by."

"Yes." Meagan remained seated. "Thanks for coming by."

Doug walked his mountain mistress to the door. At the threshold, in Meagan's blind spot, Luisa reached into her jacket pocket and removed a small white envelope. She pressed it into his hand and squeezed his fingers, then turned and descended the porch steps. He closed the door behind her and slipped the envelope into the front pocket of his flannel pajama bottoms.

"She's beautiful, Doug. We should have her over for dinner sometime."

Doug walked past his wife to the kitchen table. His coffee was cold. He took a sip and gazed at the slats of the back fence.

"Are you fucking her?" Meagan's voice was steady. Had she been crying, if her voice had cracked, he'd think there was hope.

"Of course not." He pulled the envelope from his pocket, saw *FIRST MATE* written on the front.

"Tell me you're not sleeping with that woman, Doug."

"I haven't slept with her, Meagan." *Shit. Haven't.* "I'm not."

Too late. Wanting to cheat on your pregnant wife and doing it were the same thing. The living room was silent. He tore open the envelope and slipped out a paper. *Gone to a better place. Suggest you do the same. Cyclops is resting his weary head.*

Weiss must have gotten to a doctor in Susanville or Sacramento. Doug wondered if they'd been able to save the eye. He read on. *Maybe we'll see you in the promised land. Good luck to you and the liftie. Hope we can all get the pirate crew back together for another voyage. Burn the shit out of this letter.*

Snowshoe and Freeheel were on their way north. The bunker crew had always talked of an epic backcountry trip in the Bugaboos or the Chugach. He hoped they'd make it.

"Doug?" Meagan's voice had softened.

"Meg?" He put the note back in his pocket and returned to the living room.

"What's the letter say?"

"It's not what you think, Meg." He weighed his options. Was it better to let his wife think he'd cheated on her or that he was a wanted terrorist? Except both were true.

"Did you and that girl blow up the mountain last night?"

Doug walked into the living room and found his wife curled around her body pillow on the couch, staring out the front window toward the mountains. It had started to snow.

TRADING UP

Tommy Hentzl unlocked the accordion cage that fanned across the front door of his store with one of a jumble of keys on the ring clutched in his fist. He used another key to turn on the motor that lifted the metal rollup doors covering the windows, revealing the familiar face of his shop. A white pearl-inlaid electric guitar hung diagonally across the front window above a large Peavey amplifier. Glass-encased shelves presented several solid gold wedding bands, a Naval Academy class ring, eight pairs of velvet-boxed cufflinks, and various diamond and pearl rings, earrings, and pendants. Six windows with neon signs fronted Virginia Street. A pull on the small chains hanging from each sign launched electrons, exciting the gas inside, starting the familiar buzzing glow. The tubes had been expertly bent by heat into chains of unbroken letters: PAWNSHOP JEWELRY TSHIRTS CA$H COINS LOANS

Tommy lit each word and pulled the last chain, which hung in the transom window over the doorway.

OPEN

As the sign hummed on, Tommy's sigh turned into a ragged cough. He would be opening the store for another week. Then he would retire. Most people blamed his deteriorating heart and lungs on his constant smoking, but Tommy knew it was this shop that had eroded his vitality.

He walked to the back of the store, past a long glass counter containing pistols and handguns of all makes and types. Another set of keys let him into the fortified area at the back of the building, where he unlocked the safe and turned on the lights to his small office—the desk was piled with scrawled loan application forms and appraisal sheets. He pulled a small pair of horn-rimmed glasses from the pocket of his sport coat and balanced them in their familiar resting place on the ball-shaped tip of his nose.

Ten minutes later, he heard a high-pitched beep. His nephew, Eric, didn't come in until eleven on Saturdays, and it seemed early for his first customer, but Tommy enjoyed company during the slow hours. Tourists, bums, fences, tweakers, losers, and assorted freaks always made for good conversation.

"Good morning." Tommy spoke loudly as he made his way from the back of the store. "How may I help you?"

"Just looking." The man was dressed in blue jeans, T-shirt, white tennis shoes, and a leather fanny pack. Tommy sized him up. Tourist. In town with his wife, and staying at one of the casinos across the street. Up early. Wife still in bed. Wandering downtown until she is up and they can go to breakfast together. Might buy T-shirts, tools, or possibly electronics. No guns or housewares.

"Just let me know if you see anything that interests you. Our T-shirts are three for ten dollars if you're interested, and I just got a big load of power tools in from a local contractor—really nice stuff if you have a workshop or something."

"Thanks." The man seemed hesitant to carry on a morning conversation. "I'll check it out."

Tommy noticed a large ring on the man's right hand and a wedding band on his left. The big ring was gold, its oval face embedded with a large piece of shiny black onyx in which was centered another square of gold framing a small diamond.

"That's an interesting ring. I'll give you a free appraisal."

"I'm not interested in selling it."

"That's not a problem. Some people come in and get them appraised for their insurance company. Some are just curious to see if they got a good deal on something. You never know what you might find out."

"Okay. You talked me into it." The man smiled at him and twisted at the ring, working it off his thick finger. Tommy turned on a high-powered lamp on top of the jewelry counter and fitted a visor with a loupe over his head. This jeweler getup was all for show.

Tommy took a deep breath and fingered the ring. Examining it through the magnification lens of his jeweler's loupe, he felt the warmth of the man's finger on the metal. While pretending to look at the diamond, he closed his eyes and focused inward. *This man is the original owner. Worn often, perhaps only removed for hand washings and manual labor. He does much of both. A flash of pain and guilt. Violence in the ring, first once, then several times. The fleshy parchment of skin suspended over the bones of a woman's cheek. The ring strikes thinning flesh, splitting it open against the thick brow bone above her eye socket. The inset diamond drives into a woman's jawbone. The inside of the band speaks of thin dyed-blonde strands trapped between the ring and the man's finger when he pulls a woman's hair.* Tommy's heart twisted beneath his breastbone.

The Taj Mahal Pawnbrokers shop had been in the Hentzl family for three generations. Tommy's dad and Uncle George were the original partners, and the shop now belonged to Tommy and his nephew, Eric, who ran the business end of things, including the internet auction site. Tommy was in charge of inventory and appraisals. Pawnshops had always been a great business in downtown Reno. There was never a shortage of people who were hard up—and people who needed money always seemed to have stuff. Whether they came by it legally or not was never a concern for the Hentzls. It had always been part of the local lore that folks made a pretty good living fishing wedding rings out of the Truckee River under the Virginia Street Bridge three blocks south of the Taj. But most rings attached to broken promises never went into the river. They ended up in shops like Tommy's. People often let their emotions get the best of them, but not when there was a sizeable refund available for a bad investment.

Eric came in at 9:30, carrying a tray with three large waxed-cardboard coffee cups. Tommy always drank two of them, black, while they were still hot.

"Morning, Uncle Tommy."

"You're in early."

"We've got a lot to go over. You said it yourself. Did you bring them?" Eric smiled as he took two cups of coffee from the egg carton tray and handed them, one at a time, to Tommy. It had been years since the old man had been allowed to smoke in the shop, and Eric knew Tommy needed a constant flow of hot coffee to keep him from going nuts in between smoke breaks in the alley out back.

"They're in the back. I'll show them to you later." Tommy had promised he would turn over his personal files to his nephew. There were several huge metal cabinets back in the pawnshop office containing the required customer fingerprints and all of the gun licensing paperwork, but Tommy had always kept his own set of files that he promised to share with Eric now that the younger Hentzl was taking over. These were the only tangible evidence of the abilities Tommy had developed. The manila folders were stuffed with yellowed news clippings, property sheets, and scant memorabilia, records of the lives of objects Tommy had cared for over the years. To anyone else, these would look like a morbid scrapbook of cold, journalistic prose and mundane property entries. To Tommy, the curled edges were electric with pain and suffering. An old manila folder would sear his fingers with its record of an abused stepchild, a cruel man's hands raising hidden welts on the child's back. The carbon-blue words of an old property sheet would be obscured from Tommy's vision by the blood stains of a sterling-plated flask that had cut and scarred the face of a sadistic miser's hapless business partner.

Against his uncle's advice, but with his grudging consent, Eric planned to sell the downtown property and build an ugly stucco cube on the south end of town, wedged between a drive-through coffee hut and an enormous auto parts chain store. He still needed a small physical place to sell guns and jewelry, but otherwise he intended to move all of the stock through an online, auction-based store. Tommy knew that the ether of the computer-connected world would disable his ability to divine anything about his customers, rendering him nothing more than another pawnshop owner. Today he intended to make his pitch to Eric to keep the downtown shop open two more years and let Tommy stay on as an appraiser. That should be long enough to clear out all *his* inventory, see it into good homes.

Eric nodded a hello at the fanny pack man, who was still weaving through the display cases and shelves designed on the same trapping principal as the banks of slot machines in the buildings across the street. It was impossible for a Taj Mahal customer to walk more than four steps in any direction without running into a perpendicularly placed display case. From the perspective of the overhead video camera, the store was a labyrinth. Browsers and patrons wandered through the maze without question, just as they did on the casino floors a few hundred feet away. The younger Hentzl made his way to the back of the store and closed himself in his closet-sized office to check on the Taj Mahal's overnight take from the online auctions.

Tommy could tell that the man was going to browse for a while. The customer was drawn toward the power tools, and Tommy moved to the other side of the store to give him space.

As he wandered amongst the stock, Tommy thought of how many of the items in the always changing collection were rarely, if ever, used for their original purpose. He fingered an ashtray that sat, ignored by customers, on a high shelf. *The white ceramic dish is cool but the two hands that hold it burn with anger. The arms work in a pumping frenzy as the heavy, ash-stained receptacle slams repeatedly into a man's skull. The beaten man mumbles facedown on a large oak desk. Each thrust pulverizes bone and shifts a dark brown toupee that's eventually worn down into a strip of fur mashed into the caved-in mass of scalp, bone and brain.*

Tommy turned to the little housewares section of the store and ran his hands over several kitchen appliances, pausing on a professional mixer. *Two men hold someone in the white-buttoned shirt of a sous chef in an otherwise empty kitchen. One man clutches the chef by a thin wrist, forcing his hand into a stainless steel mixing bowl in which sits the coated metal blade of an industrial mixer, still slagged with a rime of flour and egg whites. The second man immobilizes the torso of the chef. The control knob of the mixer moves from "Off" to "10." The motor whines to life. The chef screams and the first two fingers on his right hand grind in the gyrations of the spinning blade and realign themselves along the same odd axis.*

Tommy moved away from the small housewares area and passed an entire display case of cameras that had captured moments Tommy wished no one would ever have to see.

He couldn't believe how many things in the shop had been

inserted into one bodily orifice or another—he was even more surprised at how often it was done (and received) with love—or at least consent, if not pure manic desire.

In the sporting goods corner rested a hardly used pair of Reno-made Moment skis. The spatula-square tips and psychedelic graphics of the limited-edition topsheets made them a much-wanted item, and Eric had been begging to sell them online, but Tommy had been hanging on to them. They'd been part of an ill-planned bombing scheme trying to keep Tamarack Ridge a locals-only resort, and he'd yet to have a customer worthy of them. Next to the skis stood a golf putter with an oddly shaped hammerhead whose soft gripped handle had been lubed by a dark-haired woman and inserted into the willing ass end of a certain weatherman who appeared on the black and white screen of Tommy's tiny office TV every weekday morning. Out of common courtesy to his customers, Tommy had a friend of his at a golf shop re-grip the putter, but still the image lingered.

If it weren't necessary for him to read objects with his bare skin, he would have worn latex gloves around the shop. This secret knowledge had cured Tommy of one of his personal habits and led him to another. Until he had worked in the shop he had quite an oral fixation—now he was smoking cigarettes or drinking coffee to avoid chewing on pens and other innocuous objects that had led hidden lives elsewhere.

Tommy spent several hours every day rearranging all the items in the shop intuitively. First, he moved to the glass case containing handguns. They were always displayed with the barrels facing out toward the customers. He left the Glocks in a row of their own on the second shelf, and grabbed a beautiful Smith and Wesson revolver, moving it to the top of the display rack. The trigger was hot with rage and fear, although as he grasped it, Tommy could tell that it hadn't been fired in that angry state—but it had come close. He decided he wouldn't bother moving it into the "trouble" section of the case, which contained a starter's pistol that had stuck up three convenience stores and a pet shop, a revolver that had been used in two consecutive suicides, and a nine-millimeter pistol that had never been fired but had raised countless welts, broken a jaw, smashed an orbital bone, and removed three teeth courtesy of a street thug who favored pistol whipping whores and junkies.

As he passed through his store, the cumulative weight of these sensory snuff films pressed on Tommy's chest. Seeing just once what people did to one another, people he shared the streets and air of the city with, was too much. But Tommy had to see it constantly; he walked through aisles of pain, fear, and apathy. And new things always came in the door, and with them new images, sensations, and memories.

Tommy took a long, slow breath to counter the squeezing behind his breastbone and began adjusting the knives in the adjacent display counter. A sixteen-inch dagger with a dragon's head on the hilt, a faux orange jewel shoved in its mouth, had been owned by a collector, ordered from the back of a sci-fi magazine, and was only unsheathed to show other collectors. Most of the dangerous-looking weapons in this case had never cut, stabbed, or even been waved in the air as a mortal warning. Most had hung on walls or been hidden under beds to show school friends or used as awkward and misguided attempts to impress a date.

Tommy's hand ran across several knives that felt of warm vitality. The first was a large bone-handled hunting knife. Grasping it, he felt the stickiness of congealing blood oozing over the margin of the guard and onto his exposed fingers. There was a great deal of exhilaration and adrenaline but no anger here—this knife had been used to skin and gut animals, deer and once a bear, but it had never injured a human being.

Finally, he opened the last case. This was his private reserve. He reached in, and his hand found the handle of a knife that burned with blood and anger. *Two men fight in a Fourth Street motel room.* From the flashing glimpses, Tommy guessed that this was some sort of dispute over drugs and money. That neither man held the knife perplexed Tommy until the image of a woman appeared—*crouched behind the bathroom door, she clutches this knife in her fist. As one man begins choking the other, she lunges from her hiding place and stabs the attacker in the right shoulder blade—he screams and arches his back, landing face up on the filthy motel carpet. She dives at him, lodging the blade just below his left clavicle. The blade holds fast. She pulls heavily to free it. The man rolls twice across the floor and makes it to his knees near the door, pulling himself up using the knob and fleeing the room, leaving a trail of blood.* Tommy knew that this blade would never be traced back here—that man may have gone to the Washoe Medical Center ER, but he never would have told the cops his story.

He moved the knife into the trouble case. He would have to be careful whom he let purchase it; Tommy always tried to let things out the door with someone who needed a little help making the best of a bad situation. Certain items had a legacy of empowering their new owners in violent, amoral ways. He knew he didn't always make the right call—but he did his best.

When Tommy first began working for his dad and brother, he tried to keep things that had been used in crimes (moral or legal) out of his store. He would refuse to accept anything that gave off a destructive vibe—but then he started to notice something. The most brutal objects came back through the door again and again—with more blood and pain emanating from them each time. After months of this, he decided that he would trade in these items after all. He couldn't keep them out of circulation, so he might as well get them into the hands of people who might bring balance to the play of things that happened just outside his door.

He'd always taken back into the shop things that had helped those who needed it most. There was a sterling silver Tiffany and Company baby rattle sitting in the jewelry case in its familiar light blue box. It first made its way in the door with a young woman looking to unload dozens of brand new gifts from her baby shower. Tommy didn't have much of a market for car seats, bottle warmers, and blankets, but he gave the young woman fifty dollars for the rattle. When she hurried out with her cash, Tommy removed the rattle from the box. While feeling its cool smoothness in his hand, he realized that she had never been pregnant. After the expectant grandmother had invited all of her well-heeled friends for a shower, the pretend pregnancy ended in a faux miscarriage and all of the items were sold for cash.

It turned out that the rattle was something of a good luck charm. Women in particular were drawn to it, and it seemed to bring them much-needed small fortunes. One young woman brought it back to the store with a nice set of socket wrenches and a flat screen television after her boyfriend, who was fond of beating her, was sent to prison for ten years after killing a pedestrian in a hit and run DUI. Another woman, who had been on a long run of bad luck, left Tommy's shop with the rattle after he had used his charm to convince her to buy it. She had it in her coat pocket two days later when she went for a job interview at a law firm and brought it back to Tommy after she had been hired. He gave her fifty dollars cash for it and told her to use the money to celebrate.

These items would not always be used for good—Tommy harbored no naïve notions about this—but they might be used to give back some of the pain and suffering to abusers, manipulators, and cheats. Tommy was always careful about letting out items that had killed, assaulted, or intimidated, but he would occasionally entrust them to those who needed an advocate, a friend—a guardian. If given to the right customer, many of these inanimate orphans never made their way back to the shop. Funny how the foster charges displayed on these shelves were more likely to end up in the Truckee River than any recent divorcee's wedding band.

"I've got a great deal on something for your wife," Tommy found himself saying to his only early morning customer. "Surprise her, she won't expect it."

"How'd you know I was married?" the man with the onyx ring asked. Tommy pointed to the small wedding band still on the man's left hand. He walked to the end of the jewelry display case, flipping the loupe up above his head. He unlocked the case and pulled out the flat velvet box that contained women's rings. He already knew which one he wanted. It had belonged to a woman who had left her husband, pawned all of the jewelry he had given her, and used the money for a plane ticket to a new, simple life abroad. From what he could tell about this morning's customer, Tommy figured this man's wife could use a little prodding in the line of domestic separation and the start of a new life that didn't involve beatings.

"I'll give you a special deal on it."

"I'm not interested."

"Your wife doesn't like jewelry?" Tommy gestured along the top of the case with one arm like a game show girl displaying prizes.

The man laughed.

Tommy picked up the small ring he selected and held it toward the man. "I'll give you the ring for fifty."

"Not interested. I just came in to kill time."

Tommy considered the man. He had a pot belly—athletic gear was out of the question. Tommy had noticed that his knuckles were scarred and the palms of his hands were calloused.

"Tell you what," Tommy smiled. "Make me an offer on one of our power tools and I'll see what I can do to throw the ring in, too."

Ten minutes later the man walked out with the ring and a Bosch router—part of a large lot of power tools that had made its way into the shop during the devastating bankruptcy of a local contractor who later placed his own neck on a large steel table saw, the trigger of which he had rigged with duct tape. With the precision that his job had always required, the man had managed to lay out his own death so that all he had to do was place his throat at the teeth of the circular blade and step on a jerry-rigged switch. The saw sat in the corner of the Taj Mahal's tool section. Tommy smiled and wondered if the router would be contested in the divorce settlement. He wished he could have sold the man the saw, too, but Tommy had grown more patient in his older years. He had done enough for the day.

Tommy knocked on his nephew's door.

"Are you ready?"

"Sure, Uncle Tommy. Let's see what you've been hoarding all these years."

"Even you won't live long enough to see it all, Eric." Tommy saw his brother's face hidden somewhere behind his nephew's eyes. "Come in my office and leave the door open in case anyone comes in the shop."

Eric followed his uncle to the disheveled office next door. In the middle of the floor sat a hand-truck. Most of its grey paint had been beaten off and replaced by scabs of rust. Sitting on the thin steel lip was a pocked aluminum file cabinet. Tommy slid the smooth metal clasp with his thumb and pulled the long top drawer toward them. The inventory was not organized by type or date of purchase. Instead, the words on the file tabs bore Tommy's neat block printing: DEATH, DISMEMBERMENT, DIVORCE, EXTORTION, FORNICATION, INTERROGATION, JUSTICE.

Tommy had always loved the Taj Mahal because it was one of the few true marketplaces in town. Items were exchanged for money, and the money and items changed hands often. He liked to think it was one of the only places in Reno where this happened in the open. Across Virginia Street where the Mother Lode Casino towered over the pawnshop amongst a neon-clad platoon of properties stretching north and south for a mile, the money just went in one direction. Their painted and sculpted facades depicted a gold-mining boomtown, a big top circus, a Hollywood movie studio, and a Victorian railroad station. Inside, all that money went across the tables, into the slot, into the till and upstairs. It was like a waterfall in reverse, all that money cascading upward where it was counted and bundled and hurried away in secret. There were no items exchanged for the money. Just a promise of chance. It was an illusion, a faint glimmer of hope. But the money always made its way upstairs.

"I remember the year you were born." Tommy pulled three files at random out of the drawer and tossed them on his huge aluminum desk—a surplus piece from the original Brown Elementary School, now boarded up next to a freeway onramp.

"Things were tough downtown then. Everybody wanted twenty bucks, no matter what they brought in. Diamond pendant—twenty bucks. Power drill—twenty bucks. Guys would come in and try to pawn their goddamn shoes for twenty bucks. You know what cost twenty bucks back in 1973?"

"A Fulton Alley hand-job?"

"Two things. The first was a pair of roundtrip bus tickets to Sacramento. The second was a speedball—cocaine and heroin. Your dad couldn't tell who was gonna spend it on what. It drove him nuts. Me, I could always tell. That's when I realized what I can do."

Tommy opened the top folder on his desk. It had been in the "EXTORTION" file. Instead of a name on the manila tab, Tommy had written "Minolta SLR 1977."

Eric pulled over a small aluminum folding chair. He'd dropped the seat and spread the skinny, tubed legs apart when his uncle grabbed his sleeve.

"Come with me." Tommy was already half way out the door of his office.

He walked over to the electronics area and unlocked one of the glass display cases. There, hidden from view under the bottom shelf, was an ancient black Minolta single-lens reflex, a 35 mm film camera. Tommy grabbed it by the lens and handed it to Eric. It was cold and covered in dust. The two men walked back to the office and Tommy took the camera from his nephew. He aimed it at Eric, peeping at the young man's curious face through the small glass window.

"Yes," Tommy nodded, clicking the trigger, "I remember this camera. You must've been just a kid." Touching the camera again for the first time in years, Tommy saw his younger self and his brother George in the heady days of the Taj Mahal.

The woman had entered the shop early on a Friday afternoon. Tommy and George were getting ready for the four o'clock rush. Payday always brought in a steady stream of construction workers, day laborers, machinists, cashiers, and salesmen trying to get their stuff out of hock. They would cash their checks across the street at the Mother Lode and then, if they managed to find the door out of the casino with cash still in hand, they would walk, squinting in the sunlight, across Virginia Street and into the Taj Mahal. If they couldn't get their stuff back, there was always somebody else's shit they could buy.

George greeted her first. Tommy looked up when he heard her voice—raspy, deep for a woman, but something in its timbre made the hair across the top of Tommy's shoulders tingle. She was much younger than her voice, as if an aging character actress had dubbed lines over a French starlet for an art house film.

"How can I help you?" Tommy stepped toward the door from his place between the gun counters.

"I wanted to see how much I could get for this." She held up a slender hand, the skin dark, not tan. Hanging loose on her skinny forearm was a man's watch. Expensive.

"The camera first belonged to a guy named Z.D. Nyack. He had a pretty good business going as an unlicensed investigator. He did a lot of work for the casinos, helped Miles Jay put together a binder of habits and peculiarities of all the pit bosses, dealers, banquet captains, and front service managers in town. Nyack had a telephoto for the Minolta, and he used it to take pictures of husbands schlepping girlfriends when he was freelancing for unhappy wives. He made a pile of money in the heyday of the divorce boom," Tommy explained to Eric.

"So Nyack brought the camera in here?"

"No. Z.D. was found dead in the Stagecoach Inn on Fourth Street. A security guard friend of his brought me Nyack's things to raise some money for a burial plot for the guy."

"So the guard told you the story of the camera." Eric couldn't understand why the provenance of these items was so important to his uncle. It wasn't like they were dealing in priceless antiques.

"No." Tommy held the camera to his eye again and framed his nephew against the grey background of his office wall.

"The camera told me all I needed to know."

"A talking camera, Uncle Tommy? I'm glad you're getting out of the business, old man." Eric laughed and patted his uncle on the shoulder.

Tommy coughed. Sputum rattled inside his ribcage until he dislodged it, leaning forward and spitting the gummy mass into a paper cup from his desk.

"That's what these files are about. Everything in here has its secrets, Eric. For some reason, many of them have decided to share themselves with me. I don't know how, and I don't know why—but for the past thirty-five years it's something I've lived with. In many ways, I'm glad I won't have to deal with it anymore."

Tommy rose from his desk. His eyes stung from the alkaline liquid that seeped from their red, fleshy corners. He waited until he was through the office door to wipe them. For a moment there was a stifling quiet in the store. Then Tommy heard Eric shuffling through the long-hidden files on his desk. The entrance bell chimed as the front door opened and Tommy turned toward the customer, a skinny, paper-pale kid wearing a tank top and baggy jeans. His hair was spiked stiff with gel, and Tommy could smell sour alcohol on his breath.

"How can I help you?" Tommy looked the boy in the eyes. The boy shifted his glance away, shrugged, and then produced a small, zippered vinyl case from the oversized pocket of his jeans.

"I wanted to see what I could get for this. A hundred fifty bucks?"

Tommy held out his hand, and the boy handed him the pouch, still avoiding Tommy's gaze. The young man shrank back, and Tommy realized that his much larger nephew had emerged from his office to stand behind him.

Tommy unzipped the pouch. A GPS receiver, a cigarette

lighter plug, and a suction cup windshield mount nestled inside. The kind of stuff rental car companies used as upsells. Eric's voice was firm and reassuring. "If you don't want us to call the cops, walk out of here now and we won't ask any questions."

"Man, I don't know what the fuck you're talking about!" The boy moved a step toward Tommy, grabbed the pouch, and turned out the door. As soon as he hit the sidewalk he broke into a run up Virginia Street and out of sight.

Tommy turned and looked at his nephew. Behind Eric's silver-rimmed glasses Tommy could see lines etched at the sides of his eyes. A weedy patch of thick, dark stubble covered his jawline. He still had the curly, thick hair he'd had as a boy, but otherwise Tommy felt as if he were meeting him for the first time.

"Eric," Tommy grasped his nephew's forearm.

Eric turned to look at his uncle.

Tommy spoke in a hoarse, black-lung whisper. "You'll do fine with the store. It can be a rough trade, but you're up for it."

Tommy stood in the filthy alley behind the store and reveled in the hot smoke he sucked into his lungs. A late fall chill hung around him.

Eric stood in the open doorway.

"Uncle Tommy, what happened with Nyack's camera?"

Tommy remembered looking through the viewfinder when it had come into the shop. He could see his own store through the tiny window, sure, but other images kept flashing through his brain. *Grainy. Monochromatic. Passenger sedans sit in suburban driveways; men in business suits greet one another, and are admitted into midafternoon homes by housewives; cars park in front of the Palomino and Mustang Ranches.* Tommy even recognized one of the downtown pit bosses—*a series of stills of him entering the men's room at Fisherman's Park with a young male hustler.* They sure as hell weren't fishing buddies.

Eric interrupted. "So you were imagining what he must have taken pictures of. For the job."

"I didn't imagine them, Eric. They were the damn pictures this camera had taken. I could see the prints, contact sheets, negative strips. Everything. The camera was giving me everything."

Eric laughed. "I think you've been at this a bit too long."

Tommy took another drag on his cigarette. He saw the girl walk in the store thirty years ago, a huge men's watch hanging halfway up to her elbow.

Beautiful. Young. Italian, Hispanic, or perhaps Basque. Yes, Basque. Obviously not her watch, but not a boyfriend's either. Stolen. But she's not a thief. Nervous as hell.

Tommy spoke to her in a soft, firm voice. "Let me have a look at it."

She slid the metal band off her arm without unclasping it. It was heavy. Not a knockoff. He could still feel her heat on the band. She was angry, she had taken it from the owner's desk. She wanted to get back at him for something. There was another woman's touch on the watch, too. Tommy flipped the watch over, revealing an inscription on the back: *D.S. With love always Leah*

"I take it you're not Leah?"

In the end, Tommy talked her out of pawning the watch. Instead, he gave her the camera—told her she would figure out what to do with it, and when she was done with it she could bring it back to him.

"What happened to her?"

Tommy threw the nub of his cigarette into the alley and stabbed at it with a shoe heel. He re-entered the store and headed for his office, Eric following. The camera file still sat on top of his desk.

"Here you go." He handed Eric a piss-colored newspaper clipping from halfway through the pile. It was a story about the Washoe County District Attorney, who'd been brought up on corruption and racketeering charges. The accompanying photo was grainy, taken with a telephoto lens from some distance. It showed the D.A., Donald Swift, sitting down for cocktails with three well-dressed men. The photo caption identified two of the three as having been blacklisted from Nevada casinos for their involvement in organized crime. The photo byline read "Anonymous, Special to the Reno Evening Gazette."

Tommy and Eric spent hours poring through the files, finishing "JUSTICE" at 7:15 that evening, almost an hour after closing.

"Thanks, Uncle Tommy." Exhaustion wearied Eric's voice, though he'd clearly been amused by the stories the thick "FORNICATION" folder had produced.

"I just wanted to make sure you knew about what's out there on those shelves. What it all means. What you do with it is up to you." Tommy's voice was strained. He thought he'd be relieved, passing along the burdens of his gift to his successor, but showing his files to Eric had been a mistake.

Tommy had seen Eric roll his eyes and smirk several times as they'd pored over the files, interrupted only by Tommy's cigarette breaks and the buzzer of the door alerting them to customers. It was the same dismissive look the kid had when his dad George, Tommy's own brother, used to sputter nonsense through the empty fog of his dementia.

"Give me a year, Eric."

"Uncle Tommy. We agreed. You can't keep doing this. You need to take care of yourself." Eric didn't want to watch another Hentzl lose his mind in the little maze of the store.

"I'm not asking you to hold off on your plans. Talk to

the realtor. Draw up a contract to list the building. Do your computer thing." Tommy opened the bottom drawer of the file cabinet and pulled out an overstuffed plastic bag, setting it on the desk. He pulled the sealed top open and took out a handful of old-fashioned paper price tags, each with a reinforced paper ring through which ran a loop of twine.

"What's all that, Uncle Tommy? You know we put bar code inventory tags on everything now. I've got it taken care of. I have a database that keeps track of what's selling, and at what price. Those tags are old school."

"So am I." Tommy smiled.

"What's with the tags, Uncle Tommy?"

"Give me a week and a year."

"For what?"

"My inventory. There's not much of it left." Tommy stood up and left the office, returning to the miniature alleyways of the store. Eric followed him out and watched the old man shuffle around a glass display case.

"Give me a week to price and label everything…unique." Tommy took one of the blue tags and wrapped the string around the binding of one of the Moment skis. He touched the toe piece and was transported to the woods of Tamarack Peak.

An explosion. A blizzard in reverse as snow and then dirt and tree limbs float skyward, then plummet to the earth. Debris. An eyeball, dangles from an optic nerve. A marriage in peril. Skis, boots, a bench made of snowboards, loaded into a camper shell.

"Uncle Tommy?"

He let go of the skis and made his way across the store, pulling another label from the bag.

"Don't make me call my lawyer friend, Eric. Don't make me draft up a will. I don't want to set up stipulations on you or the store. Just promise me this. Sell the store. Sell everything on the computer. Just let me find a good home for my blue tagged merchandise. I won't take anything else in."

"Promise me, Uncle Tommy?"

"Promise *me*, Eric."

Uncle and nephew shook hands.

When Tommy walked out the door that night, he felt he'd done all he could for his little city. He was proud that he had kept Reno's secrets all these years.

At half past ten that night, the secrets died with Tommy. His heart, the muscle that had endured so much with him, stopped for good. The denizens of the Taj Mahal Pawn, Loan & Jewelry had no one left to tell their stories or chart their course in the world.

PENNED

It hadn't rained for three weeks. Heat seared the wide, flat saucer of the Great Basin, bending the light in a phantasm of waves, which, in their shimmer, obliterated the image of anything still inhabiting the barren ground. It was sweltering in the trailer. Iago stamped his hooves and rocked against the hot metal sides. A man approached, his boots crunching on the small rocks of the dirt road. The man clicked his mouth as he came alongside. Iago ululated in return.

A thin, slick coat of sweat was already forming on his withers and he blinked as he picked his way down the short ramp of the trailer into the white-hot sunlight. The flying machine chopped at the air in the distance, and below it, a cloud of dust rose from the unseen herd. They were headed his way. It was time to work.

A pair of huge fences seemed to run off forever into the desert. Here, where he stood, they narrowed, and he could not shuffle in either direction without brushing his haunches against them. As they moved away from him they widened into a canyon, enough for an entire herd to move through abreast. He could smell the perfume of the sagebrush, and to his right he could hear a half-dozen human voices, hidden behind jute-covered corral panels. He heard his name whispered, and the other thing they called him—*Judas*. Behind him, the chutes and corrals and human things were all but invisible.

The man in the white straw hat stood close to Iago, and

the horse clenched the brim of the hat between his teeth and nibbled on it until the man slapped him on the side of the neck with a long, skinny flag, and then walked him far out onto the desert floor and toward the vibrations of the approaching herd. Once Iago was clear of the wing-like fencing of the horse trap and onto the open range, the man pulled the hat from his head and ducked into a large patch of sagebrush, lying prone in the cover.

Iago turned toward the cloud of dust pouring from behind a small rock-covered hill. To lead the flighty herd toward the corrals, he would have to wait for the stallion at the front, nudging him withers to withers and boxing him toward the camouflaged funnel the people had spent the morning setting up. If the stallion turned or spooked at the last minute, the herd would follow him back to the open range.

Iago flicked his head up and down, eager to run alongside the herd and do as he'd been taught—lead the stallion into the narrowing walls of jute-covered steel corral panels and into the chute to the pens beyond. This was where instinct trumped his training, and the gelding longed to run with the herd, if only for a moment.

He could feel the approaching horses—the musky smell of the females and the excited call of the stallion. The vibration of the helicopter blades beating at the air washed across him, and he blinked away the dust and grit that spun into his face.

Iago turned his body and placed his rump to the herd as the stallion came into view, the rest strung out behind. He was enormous—a buckskin with a thick black stripe that ran the length of his spine, an outward sign of his lineage going back to the horses of the conquistadors who had crossed this continent almost 600 years ago. Despite the lead animal's size, Iago could see festering wounds on the stallion's flanks, his ribs pushing outward through his ragged coat.

Doing his best to shock the stallion into the trap, Iago focused on a sore on the beast's side and drove his muzzle deep into the raw fissure. The stallion whinnied and turned toward the Judas horse without breaking stride, snapping at the ginger gelding and grinding his teeth while his wild eyes marked this unexpected traitor.

Iago swiftly drove himself along the big stallion's flanks and shoved his head toward the ribs, forcing the yellow and black leader to the left toward the maw of the waiting pens. With the force of the herd fleeing in terror from the flying machine now hovering a few feet above them and the prada harassing his flanks, the stallion, spooked and frenzied, galloped down the mouth of the trap, into the head of the chute, and toward the back of the pen, confused by the flapping walls of fabric, exhausted and thirsty. He turned to watch the rest of his herd, no longer free, follow him without a fight into the makeshift corral.

The heavy sound of the metal gate slamming always reminded him he was captive. Even while on his way out into the late September heat of a Nevada Indian summer, Hank Redente was aware that his life was spent in a series of cages and corrals. It was a few months until the next open adoption, and the men of the Ormsby Conservation Camp Horse Gentling Program had a lot of work to get to.

He heard a familiar voice yell from across the lawn in front of the dorms.

"Hank the Shank! Living large in the OCC."

Demetrius Bryant was the only black inmate working in the horse program, a fact that was never overlooked and the topic of frequent ball-busting by the white, Hispanic, and Native American inmates who made up the bulk of the wranglers in the minimum security camp slung in the shadow of the hulking ruins of the maximum security prison next door, still operating behind its crenellated and concertinaed battlements like a high-desert Bastille.

"Dbag." Hank punched his co-worker on the arm and fell in beside him as the two men walked down the long gravel road toward the horse stalls. "I'm surprised you're here this early—they do a quick cavity search today, or are you just getting so loose in the caboose that contraband just falls out now?"

Both men tried their best to maintain a prisoner's dignity, wearing the blue cotton shirt and dungarees in as menacing a manner as possible.

The men sorted Iago out of the main corral and left him sequestered in a side pen with a small bucket of tepid water. Iago could hear the frightened whinnies of the mares and feel the confused stumbling of the herd, penned for the first time in their lives. Several of the animals were supine, hooves split and bleeding from their run across the baked pan. One of the downed animals came to rest against the fence next to him and he could see its distended eyeball scanning him. The orb spun in the socket several times and the disembodied animal chuffed—Iago could feel the breath on his fetlock—and was at once still and silent. The pupil in the now frozen eye grew large and black.

Iago pressed against the corral panel, moving away from the still horse, and neighed into the hot desert breeze.

"Easy there, fellah." Another man in a straw hat came by and patted his neck, clicking at him. After a few minutes, he stopped calming the Judas horse and unlatched the gate. "Let's get you into the trailer and out of this circus." He slipped a halter over Iago's muzzle and led him around the outside of the corral. Iago sulked behind the man and loaded into the dark confined space where he would doubtless still hear the terror and confusion of the herd, but would no longer see it.

The man put a flake of hay into the trailer and closed the door behind Iago with a metallic clang.

Hank and Demetrius reached the corrals to find Estebe "Stub" Barrios already feeding the horses. The slight, olive-skinned man looked younger than his fifty-one years. He was about six feet tall and slender in his hand-tooled boots, large, flat-brimmed straw hat and button down shirt. He had his toes shoved into the slot between two of the heavy duty highway guard rails that doubled as fence panels on the ranch—the Nevada Department of Transportation having donated a huge supply of pressure-treated timber and heavy rails from a pile in some backwater DOT yard. Large plastic buckets of spare bolts lay near different corrals, ready to replace any kicked loose by a horse or stripped by the ranch hand inmates.

"Mornin', boys." The lean Basque was flaking and tossing hay over the fence, all the while eyeing the body language of the herd.

"Good morning, sir." Hank and Demetrius, like the other ten hands in the horse program, treated Stub with great respect and deference. They weren't afraid of him, but they knew that without his support and constant guidance, they'd soon be working across the pasture at the dairy farm, or worse, back in the general population in the medium or max facility that stood silhouetted in the rising sun.

"It's going to be hot today." Stub feathered a hay flake from the tines of a pitchfork into a metal feeder near a skittish mare. "Make sure you and the horses get plenty of water."

With that, he tossed the last of the feed over the fence and turned to smile at them before heading to the next pen to assess the rest of his four-legged charges.

Hank was glad Stub had seen they'd been the first two to

work this morning. He could already hear the pack of his co-workers walking past the shop and turning on the road that would take them beyond the dairy cows and out to the pens where he stood.

The two friends walked to a small construction trailer and signed in on a clipboard. They each grabbed oversized white bike helmets and strapped them over their ball caps. Hank laughed at Demetrius. Before him stood a muscled black man in prison-issued blues, capped with an enormous white dome that wouldn't look out of place on a little girl riding her bicycle at a park.

"You can fuck yourself, cowboy. I'm in no mood for your shit today." Demetrius slapped Hank's helmet so hard that a trail of little sparks spun in front of his eyes and one of his ears rang.

Today, Stub would be hand-selecting the horses that each man would be training for the next 120 days before they were auctioned to the public. Hank had his eye on a huge strawberry roan gelding that was in the pen where Stub had been feeding.

Demetrius had his eye on something else completely.

"Think Stub'll let me have that little brown one?" He pointed to the smallest horse in the corral getting pinned against the wall by the roan.

"Bay." Hank stretched his jaw and rubbed the back of his neck, trying to recover his senses from Demetrius's head slap.

"I thought we got to name 'em."

Hank laughed. "It's a bay. Not brown. Dogs are brown. Let Stub hear you talk like that and you'll end up with one of the burros."

"Shit, man. Anything I'm taller than's okay with me." Demetrius sighed and walked to the shed for a pitchfork so he could begin mucking out the pens.

The rest of the convict cowboys could be heard before they

emerged around the corner of the riding arena and into sight. They traveled in a pack of indigo jeans, light blue chino shirts, and navy vests with the horse program logo embroidered over the left breast. Most wore blue baseball caps but a few left their closely shorn hair exposed to the cool morning air.

As usual, the group was led by Ryan Gilchrest, an intense-looking kid of twenty-five with tattoos visible at both wrists and along the left side of his neck. Behind him stood Arapaho Joe—Joseph Left Hand, a slim, short Indian from Wyoming who'd been arrested in Winnemucca for breaking into trailers and stealing alcohol and prescription meds. He'd been found passed out on a plastic picnic table early one morning in a McDonald's Playland with a stolen laptop and a bottle of Jack Daniels next to his head.

"Hey! It's Evony and Ibory," cackled Antonio Vargas, #635418, felony possession of methamphetamine, grand theft auto, two to five, and the best horseman of the group.

"That's Ebony and Ivory," Hank picked up a still-warm, wet horse turd and launched it at the little Mexican. Vargas sidestepped it and lunged toward Hank as Stub emerged from nowhere and, with a glance, got the whole crew moving through their morning chores.

The wranglers who unloaded the trailer whipped wild-flags in the air to keep the horses moving—the strips of plastic bags cracked on the end of thin crops. As he clomped from the trailer into a squeeze chute, the cryptic runes of the freeze brand on the left side of his neck were logged onto a clipboard, "number 0-8-6-4…no…3. 0-8-6-3-9-1-7-2." The processing continued as the horses were sorted, assessed by a vet who'd driven out for the occasion, and led to smaller pens in groups of five or six where they were fed and watered.

"This one's feisty." The stock contractor who'd hauled

the mustangs from the large wild horse processing facility seventy miles away pointed the big roan out to Stub. "He bit my partner loading in, and kicked my finger when I slipped my hand in through the trailer slats to grab a hoof pick." The young wrangler, still holding a wild-flag, lifted his hand to show Stub a gnarled black and blue index finger that looked puffed and broken.

The horse saw the white plastic flutter in the air and lurched away, slamming into an unlatched gate that swung free from the pressure of his body. He stumbled sideways across a pile of fence posts and found himself unpenned in a flat open space. He smelled the water of a river across the fields and took off at a full gallop, away from the yells of the men growing faint behind him.

Hank and Demetrius went almost everywhere together. They'd met in the dorm six months ago, when Demetrius arrived after processing at the Fish Tank in the maximum-security unit up the road. There was an extra bed in Hank's room that had been vacated the week before by one of the firefighters in the camp who'd made it out to a halfway house.

As was customary, the men's first conversation centered around the various ways and means they'd found their way into the little six-bed room in the cinder block dorm, which could have been mistaken for a small elementary school if not for the guard towers and concertino wire.

Demetrius had been pulled over on the Vegas Strip in 2009 and LVPD had found a hastily tossed bag of cocaine on the front seat floorboard of his car.

"I got a DWB and one-to-three for something you'd be out on probation for," Demetrius explained.

"You're saying you're in here because you were Driving While Black?"

"That's right." Demetrius looked hurt.

"I think that's DWBWCIC," Hank said. "Driving While Black With Cocaine in the Car." Thinking he'd gotten the upper hand on his new dorm mate, Hank soon found he'd have to answer for his own jacket.

"What're you in for, Cowboy Hank?" Demetrius gave him a cold stare.

"Third felony DUI."

"Why're you in here and not in some program somewheres?" Demetrius smiled, coaxing the whole truth out of Hank.

"Because my third felony DUI ended up with me putting my boss's Ford F-150 in a little old lady's front bedroom."

"You drove through grandma's house?" Demetrius slapped Hank on the back and folded over in shuddering laughter.

"I swerved to keep from hitting a horse on Geiger Grade and went right into a house in Virginia Highlands."

"A wild horse?" Bryant tilted his head toward the shop and dairy barn, beyond which was a herd of Nevada mustangs.

"And if I find out which one it was, I'm gonna shank the big-toothed motherfucker." Hank pulled an imaginary shiv from the sleeve of his blue work shirt and pantomimed disemboweling a horse while Demetrius exploded in a fit of laughter that caught the attention of a guard, forcing them to move down the road to work.

The big strawberry horse was enjoying the cold, sweet water of the Carson River when he heard the first vehicle approach from downstream.

Two men holding long black sticks emerged from a white van and, from back toward the ranch, he heard the full gallop of horses. Ahead of them, kicking up a trail of dust, came a thrashed pickup truck hand-painted forest green with a garish yellow stripe running horizontal from front quarter panel to taillight. In the cab were two men, and six more piled out of the bed. One had a large rope he was already twirling above his head. As the men closed in on him from all sides, the horse dipped his muzzle into the cool river water and took a long, satisfying drink.

All twelve men sat atop a ten-foot length of guardrail at the crown of the sorting pen where Stub was expertly cutting out geldings one by one.

"Tony!"

"Yes, sir." Vargas clambered down into the pen and walked toward the head trainer, who had separated a little black four-year-old and had him standing up against the fence on the far side of the pen.

"The little black one is yours. He's gaited and will make a smooth ride for somebody who spends a lot of time riding. Let's see what you can do with him."

"Yes, sir." Antonio smiled as he approached the animal, kissing at the air and clicking his tongue to the roof of his mouth. The horse bobbed its head as he neared, but it let him get close enough to pat along the nape of its neck.

"Ryan!"

"Yeah, Stub!" Gilchrest had taken off his vest and rolled up the sleeves of his work shirt, revealing the breadth and detail of the tattoos that continued under the bulging blue cloth.

"The roan is yours, if you think you can handle him." Stub moved toward the largest horse in the pen. It didn't flinch.

The men on the fence whistled and trash talked Gilchrest as he proudly walked toward Stub and his new project. Hank sat, dumbfounded, as he realized the horse he'd planned on training for the next four months would not be his.

"You can have the brown one...I mean the...bay one," Demetrius whispered to Hank as a consolation.

As Gilchrest approached the big gelding, the horse turned his head up toward the fence and nickered. The inmate moved to work his way up the horse's muscular left side just as the animal shuffled his back feet, twisted his hips toward the man, and let go with a flying double kick that sent the tattooed inmate flying across the pen to ragdoll face up in the soft dirt.

Twelve men came off the fence at once, but Stub got to him first. Gilchrest was out cold and his face was a mess of blood, swollen flesh, and a few teeth still tenuously attached to their owner's gums.

Six minutes later, the men loaded Ryan Gilchrest in the back end of a white utility van and watched as two guards jumped in and sped away toward the gate and the maximum-security prison infirmary beyond.

"Hank!"

Stub had moved them all back into the pen once the van had taken Gilchrest away. He was standing again by the big roan.

"Yeah, Stub?" Hank's hands were shaking as he looked at the pool of blood coagulating where his fellow inmate had lain immobile a few minutes before.

"The roan is yours. Come over here and introduce yourself to him."

It was a long walk across the pen.

The next morning, Demetrius snuck out of the dorm early to avoid waking his roommates. He checked out for work detail, exited the security gate that separated the living quarters from the ranch, and made his way to the manager's office to transfer out of the horse program.

Hank awoke soon after to find his roommate already gone. He stuffed his legs into his dungarees and sprinted down the gravel road past the shop and the dairy cows. When he arrived at the manager's trailer, he could see Demetrius framed in the open doorway, already filling out paperwork. Hank climbed the three stairs and entered the little trailer.

"What're you doing, D?"

"I'm not working with killers, Hank." Demetrius fixed his eyes on the buttons of his blue shirt.

"Mr. Redente. Thanks for getting here so early today." The ranch manager was one of the calmest, most soft-spoken men Hank had ever met. Jeff Exline was clearly not going to try to convince Demetrius to stay. He would consider the request, file the paperwork, and let the men make whatever decisions they felt they needed to.

"It looks like we're going to have two new openings. I'll post the jobs this afternoon, but if you know of someone who might be a fit, let me know and I'll get their I-9s and talk to their counselors."

The wild horse program was the most sought-after rehabilitation unit in the camp, and any time someone was paroled or transferred, ten inmates applied for a single position.

"Two openings?" Hank knew the answer before the question had even tumbled out of his mouth.

"Mr. Gilchrest is not going to be able to work with horses for awhile, I'm afraid. He's broken an orbital bone, can't see out of one eye just yet, and has his jaw wired shut."

"And I ain't gonna end up like that sorry motherfucker." Demetrius was looking at Hank now. His eyes were glistening and Hank realized it was the first time he'd ever seen his friend look scared.

"What're you going to do, D?" Hank appreciated that Exline was letting him speak to his friend, the three of them wedged into the tiny office already beginning to warm from the heat of their bodies.

"I don't know, man." Demetrius stared at his own work boots, the toes just a few inches from Exline's polished cowboy boots.

"Mr. Bryant feels that he'd like to move over to the fire camp." Exline held out an application for the trustee hand crew.

"Really, D? You want to hike your ass through the woods for three days, breathing smoke and wearing five layers of clothes in the heat of the summer? You might as well just ask them to put you back in the Fish Tank and send you back to Vegas."

The high-security facility in the desert near Sin City was not high on the list of addresses wanted by the Nevada state inmates.

"Jeff," Hank turned to the manager and held out his hand, "can I have that paperwork? I'll help Demetrius look it over before he makes any rash decisions."

Exline smiled and handed over the hand crew application and the transfer request. "I'll need to know by tomorrow."

"Thanks, Jeff. We'll let you know."

"Thank you, Mr. Exline." Demetrius followed his friend out the door. The two inmates climbed down from the trailer and walked toward the horse corrals.

"You've got to ride first, DB." The two men sat in the bleachers in front of the empty dirt floor of the arena. Other men were arriving and grabbing their helmets and tools from the shed, but everyone was wandering about the yard without purpose—Stub was giving them an hour or two to shake everything off from the prior day's accident before he started dogging them to get their asses back in line.

"I can't, Hank. Not after what I seen that animal done to that man. I'm not getting near them, and I'm not getting on them."

Hank stood and walked down the front of the bleachers toward the stalls where they kept a few of the gentle horses used to train the new inmates in the program, a good percentage of whom had never ridden before.

He opened a gate and walked into the pen where he caught the eye of Danny Boy, a chestnut with a sweet disposition.

Hank gestured with one arm raised, curling his fingers toward the palm of his hand. Danny walked across the pen toward him and stuck his head over Hank's shoulder so that the man could scratch his neck and mane.

"Danny, I'd like you to meet my friend Demetrius."

The first week with the new animals was long and exhausting. Men were bitten. Men were kicked. Horses were smacked with open palms. Arapaho Joe made one round of the arena slung by his left stirrup underneath his horse, Chino, his head bouncing off the ground in time to the horse's trot.

In the middle of it all, Stub kept a cool head and mediated agreements between man and horse, working as a translator fluent in the languages of two species.

Vargas had saddled and ridden his mount, a dun mare, on the first day, and while most of the men were still doing groundwork, walking the horses in large circles with a lead rope and approaching them from both sides, tying on saddles and halters, the little Mexican was working his horse, whom he'd named Dorada, by riding her to a smooth stop, backing up, and even walking sideways in both directions.

Hank had moved his horse into a separate pen to keep him from hazing the other horses (and inmates) while the two of them gained each other's trust. The ruddy beast was surly and wicked most mornings, and Hank had dubbed him Iago, remembering the character from high school Shakespeare and the fact that the roan had betrayed everyone he'd come into contact with so far.

Demetrius rode Danny Boy with the help of the other

men. His fear had begun to subside enough that he started groundwork with his gelding.

"I'm calling him Dock," he told Hank one morning while feeding his bay. He seemed resolute in his decision to stay on with the horse program. Hank had convinced him to tear up the fire crew application after much cajoling and questioning of his black pride, his prison cred, and his manhood.

"Doc." Hank thought about it for a moment. "I like it—like the cure for what ails you. The doctor of love. What's up—"

"No, dumbass. D-O-C-K." Demetrius walked toward the horse and offered an upturned palm full of oats to his charge. He had yet to climb aboard.

"You're going nautical with the name, then." Hank didn't see any connections that made sense.

"I'm giving this horse some soul, Hank. When I get up on him, I'm gonna be whistling. Just like Otis did."

"Who in the hell is Otis?"

"Redding. Otis Redding. Don't tell me you only listen to sorry-ass country music."

"You can't be serious." Hank tugged the rope on the halter as the big strawberry horse threw its head and chuffed in annoyance.

"Dock of the Bay, my friend. That's where I'll be sittin'." Demetrius headed for the tack shed to get a saddle. Hank was still laughing as he watched his friend walk with more confidence than he'd ever seen him display in the presence of horses.

It was short lived.

Antonio showed Demetrius how to cinch the saddle and flip the stirrups up onto the seat to train the horse to stand stock-still and await commands. He said it was like setting the parking brake.

Once the horse appeared calm, Demetrius approached on

the left, whispered in Dock's ear, pulled down the stirrup, and roughly mounted, throwing his leg across the animal's back and yanking the reins for leverage.

"Let him out."

Vargas was right there alongside the greenest rider of the group.

"Give him some reins, D."

Demetrius walked Dock around the large pen, where the other men and horses were working on a combination of putting on tack, riding, and groundwork.

As Dock let himself be led to a trot around the pen, man and horse moved past Iago. Dock's ears and tail lowered as they slipped past. At the last moment, the roan leaned forward and sunk his teeth into Dock's flank. The little bay kicked, and Demetrius yanked back on the reins. Dock reared twice and regained his feet with an empty saddle. Demetrius was lying behind his horse.

Everyone but Hank laughed. Antonio glided over to Dock and slipped the reins off his neck, patting his muzzle and whispering to him in Spanish.

Stub's head appeared over the top of the guardrail.

"Bryant. Get that horse."

Demetrius picked himself off the dirt and shuffled over toward Antonio, who handed him the reins. The black man turned to look at Stub for guidance.

"Get back to work, son."

Demetrius shook his head.

"Do it now." Stub was calm but firm. He knew he had to fix both man and horse, right there and then.

"Come on, D." Antonio put a hand on the back of his coworker's vest and guided him toward the saddle.

Demetrius sighed twice, lifted his left boot to the stirrup, and, in one fluid lift and kick of his right leg, gained his seat on Dock and took the reins from Vargas. The two trotted the arena again to the cheers and whoops of the other inmates.

The horse responded to *Iago* now. It meant food and attention. He wanted to run, but not with a man on his back. He'd take a rider though, since it meant being let out of the pen. He hated the pen more than anything. The stopping, starting, turning—even the hackamores and bridles, all meant time outside the fences, and he began to accept work and its rewards.

"Iago." He moved toward the voice, hoping for a handful of oats to start his day. He smelled two men. Only one was familiar.

"Here he is, Ryan." Hank's voice was near.

A familiar face greeted him at the front of the corral fence. Next to it was another man—the face uneven, marbled purple and yellow, and puckered around one milky eye.

"Take a good look at this busted face, you red-assed sonofabitch." Iago reared from the fence, loped to the far side of the corral. Hank laughed and clicked at Iago, coaxing him back to the fence.

"Let me in there, Hank." Ryan Gilchrest unlatched the gate.

"I'll come with." Hank didn't want to referee round two between his horse and the man whose face Iago had pulverized.

Iago stayed on the far side of the pen as the man with the broken face cantered toward him. A rough pair of hands stroked his mane. When Gilchrest moved to scratch his muzzle, the horse stiffened and pulled his head to the side. Gilchrest's voice gentled and slowed, and he soon shook Hank's hand and hobbled out of the corral. Iago remained up against the fence when Hank, alone again, called to him. Iago stood at the fence a long time before he shuffled to his trainer, ears and tail low, to accept oats that'd warmed in the palm of Hank's hand.

The auction was a week away.

All the men were fine tuning their horses and choosing special tricks that would show their skills as riders, and, more importantly, the personalities and best traits of their horses.

Antonio had a full routine to show Dorada's smooth gait. She could side-pass in both directions, cut around a hat tossed on the ground and, for good measure, walk in circles kicking a giant inflatable ball with her front legs.

Dock and Demetrius had come along nicely. The bay was gentle by nature, and wanted to work. After months of eight-hour days, Demetrius was a great hand and a passable rider.

Hank had the most work to do. He'd worked Iago to their mutual exhaustion seven days a week, riding him into a lather every weekday, and still the big roan tested him and every man in the outfit, even getting the better of Stub one rainy morning.

Hank was determined that today would be their breakthrough—establishing once and for all which of the incarcerated bachelors, man or horse, would forever dominate the other. Hank figured the odds about even.

"Come on, D." Hank led Iago into the large yard between the pens where Demetrius was picking dirt out of Dock's hooves.

"'Sup, Hank?"

"We're going for a ride. You and me. Stub said we could take them to the river."

The entire group had ridden that far only a few times, and then they had Stub with them aboard Danny Boy, and two guards in a van had been parked on the frontage road along the river—just in case.

Iago kicked, stalled, and spun. He pulled his head around so quickly to nip Dock's ear that he almost pulled Hank off by the reins. He tried bucking once, started to rear twice, and mashed himself alongside a high fence of bolted guardrails.

The former ranch hand was unfazed. Each time Iago got

out of line, he corrected him gently and immediately, and by the time the two men reached the lower pasture, both horses were at a full gallop, their riders whooping and laughing.

When they returned to the main yard, all four of them were panting, lathered in sweat.

"Thanks, Hank." Demetrius held the reins in his left hand and extended his right toward his friend.

"No worries, D. It was a nice ride."

"I mean thanks for talking me into staying. You know I've been out and in twice already." This was his second stint in prison. He'd only spent two years outside inbetween. "When I get back out, I'll be back in Vegas with the same people that got me in here. I always thought I was chasing fun and living life. But when we get to come out here and turn them loose, that's freedom, man. I love this shit."

Demetrius clicked once, threw his head back in a war whoop, and kicked Dock back into a full gallop. As Hank put his heels to Iago's flanks to close the gap, he could hear Demetrius ahead of him, whistling an Otis Redding tune.

The men showed up just after dawn to clean and brush the horses. The auction preview would start soon. The arena was raked, smoothed, and dragged. Inmates scrubbed the white fiberglass bleacher seats as two pairs of guards looked on, huddled in military-style jackets against the cold of the morning.

Once the arena was spotless and the horses washed, brushed, and saddled, the men turned to one another, swiping grit and shit off the backs of denim legs and straightening vests and helmets with military regimen.

At 8:30, cars started rolling into the makeshift parking lot. One of the first vehicles in the lot was a huge diesel haul tractor without a trailer hitched behind. On the door was painted a bubble-cockpit helicopter wearing a ten-gallon hat sprouting a set of rotors. Its right skid, stylized into a skinny arm, twirled a lasso. *Airborne Livestock & Cattle Co.* was painted above the cartoon flying machine. By 9:00, all of the inmates sat astride their horses in front of the arena where potential buyers and curious onlookers milled about.

Hank must have talked to fifty people before the auctioneer mounted the small platform next to the arena—folks wanted to pet Iago and learn more about the big ruddy horse.

A BLM man in a khaki baseball hat and grey jeans spent a great deal of time talking to him about Iago. Hank recognized him from previous auctions, but he didn't know the older man with him. The latter had obviously spent plenty of time around roughstock judging by his pained gait and gnarled hands.

"How does he go over rough ground?" The older of the two inquired without so much as an introduction or a handshake.

"I've had him down to the river a couple times," Hank patted Iago's neck. The big horse bobbed his head up and down. He whinnied impatiently and raked his foreleg across the dirt. "He's as sure-footed as I've seen."

One of the last patrons to make his way down to Hank and Iago was Hank's old boss, Miles Jay. Hank had been the stock manager at the Blue Jay Ranch, Miles's exclusive enclave in south Reno, where performers who played his Mother Lode Hotel and Casino would be put up in style in Miles's ranch-house mansion. He loved stocking the corrals with exotic breeds and mustangs. It had been a Blue Jay Ranch work truck that Hank had driven into the old woman's house up on Geiger Grade.

"Mr. Jay." Hank extended his hand through the corral fence. "It's great to see you, sir."

For a septuagenarian, Miles Jay had a firm handshake. "How are you holding up, Hank? Glad to see you."

"I'm doing well, sir." Hank still felt bad that he'd caused his boss a nightmare of bad publicity that drunken night.

"Still working the horses, I see? I'm hoping to add to my collection." Miles smiled at his former employee and raised the auction catalog. Iago had been circled in thick black marker, along with at least two other horses.

"Good luck, Mr. Jay."

"You too, Hank. It was good to see you."

At 10:00, the auctioneer slipped the hands-free microphone over his neck and people took their seats. The BLM man and his companion were front row, center. The inmates trotted their horses out of the arena and into the back pasture, awaiting their turn to file in as their horses' names were called. The Ormsby Conservation Camp's debutante ball began.

Joe Left Hand thundered into the arena on Chino and put him through his paces, stopping short, backing up, and trotting in a serpentine formation around traffic safety cones.

Once he'd finished his show, the auctioneer started the bidding at $200. In a modulated, rapid-fire voice, he cajoled two middle-aged women into a bidding war for Chino. A pretty woman in cream-colored jeans and a skin-tight sweater with silver and turquoise bangles on each wrist finally won the bidding war, buying Chino for $900. She walked over to the fence at the arena-side pen to meet her new mount and talked to Joe for ten minutes while the other inmates watched him try to peek at her cleavage from his high vantage on Chino's back.

Hank walked Iago in circles in the back pen to calm the horse as they waited their turn to enter the arena. The BLM man approached Stub and Jeff near the auctioneer's platform and the three of them walked toward him.

Jeff was the first to reach the fence. "Why don't you bring Iago around back, Hank. We'd like to take a look at him."

"He's just fine, Jeff. He's sound. And ready."

"That's not what I mean, Hank. Meet us around in the yard and we'll explain."

Stub nodded from behind the two men, and Hank rode Iago through a chute and a gate, then walked him out into the lot behind the bleachers. Two guards warily eyed Hank until Jeff caught one's eye and nodded. The auctioneer's high-speed drone echoed among the empty pens and bounced off the sides of horse trailers and guardrails.

"We're going to pull Iago from the auction, Hank." Jeff's face indicated that this was not negotiable.

Hank opened his mouth to speak, but Jeff raised his hand and continued. "As you know, the BLM can request any one of our horses prior to the auction, and Mr. Gardner, who's here as a guest of the program, wants to use Iago for a Judas horse."

Hank lowered his head and stared at the pommel of Iago's saddle. His stomach churned. They were going to use his horse as BLM bait. A traitor. He'd trained a snitch horse. If the horse were a con in the max unit across the street, Iago wouldn't live longer than a week on the yard.

"Let Mr. Gardner bid for him, then." Hank had never stared down the ranch manager before.

"Mr. Gardner is a contractor with the BLM, and they have the right to pull any of our stock prior to the auction." Stub, his ever-calm self, tilted his head toward the BLM man beside him. "He's claiming Iago on Mr. Gardner's behalf." He'd dealt with wilder horses and inmates than Iago and Hank, often at the same time.

"But he's beautiful. And tough. He'll clear top dollar and you know it, Stub."

"And he doesn't belong to you, Hank." Stub took his hat off and tousled his night-black hair. "You've done a great job with him, son. But he was going out the gate this afternoon no matter what, and you don't get to pick who he goes with."

"Besides, Hank," Jeff smiled, "he gets to run all over the range instead of stuck in some trophy wife's stall with a braided tail."

Hank spent the rest of the auction in the yard with the BLM man and Larry Gardner. They checked the white freeze brand on the side of Iago's neck and looked at his legs, teeth, hooves, and eyes. The on-site vet joined them and declared Iago a stout specimen of equine health.

When they had finished, Hank walked out to the parking lot to help his co-workers get their horses loaded into the buyers' trailers. Arturo Vargas was loading Dorada into the back of an ancient single-stall rig that Hank recognized as one of the Blue Jay Ranch's. Miles had always been the cheapest rich bastard he'd known and wouldn't let an old trailer go to waste. He noticed that Demetrius was talking and laughing with Miles Jay himself, the black man's oversized bike helmet still strapped on his head.

"This gentleman bought Dock," Demetrius smiled at his friend. "For twenty-three hundred dollars!"

Miles nodded.

"He bought Dorada, too." Demetrius watched the golden mare disappearing into the trailer. "So they're picking Dock up tomorrow."

"What happened with Iago?" Miles had marked Hank's horse in the auction catalog and noticed that he'd never come up for bid.

"He's heading out next week." Hank's voice cracked. "In a BLM stock trailer." Dorada neighed in the trailer and it rocked on creaky springs. "He's gonna be a Judas horse."

Arturo latched the back of the trailer and Miles walked around the far side, pretending to be occupied with checking the tires and the hookup for the trailer brakes.

"That means we've got one more day to ride them."

Demetrius looked at Hank and then gestured to the pen where Iago and Dock ran with two others that had not been bought in the auction.

And they rode.

Past the dairy cows and the arena and the alfalfa fields. They rode past the irrigation pond and the breeding yard and the hay bales and the shop. They rode past the furthest guard tower and waved at the silhouette of the man behind the glass. They crossed the far field and down the river bank and into the river and they rode downstream to a small gravel bar.

They watered the horses and waited, in no hurry to return to the gates and pens and fences behind them. This was the farthest out they had been, and the sun on their faces and the horses beneath them—it was the freest they'd felt since they'd been here, and maybe before that.

And then they turned for home. Splashing across the shallow river, they galloped up the bank and thundered through the stretched, late afternoon shadow of the guard tower. Past the hay and the shop and the pond and the fields. They slowed at the arena, letting the horses cool down.

As they neared the pasture, the engines of the crew trucks at the fire camp burst to life and watched as distant figures grabbed heavy packs and bundled in clothes, cramming aboard the trucks. One by one the diesels roared and the trucks rolled up the driveway in a long, slow procession. It was already over eighty degrees. Demetrius looked at the trucks and looked at Hank and the horses. And he smiled.

MARK MAYNARD

Mark Maynard is a writer, editor, and journalist who teaches at Truckee Meadows Community College. He is an editor for *The Meadow* literary journal and his work has appeared in *Lunch Ticket*, *The Nottingham Review*, and in the 2012 anthology T*ahoe Blues: Short Lit on Life at the Lake*. Maynard is the recipient of the 2015 Nevada Writers Hall of Fame Silver Pen Award, and *Grind* was selected as the 2016-17 Nevada Reads book. His work has appeared in *The Reno News* and *Review* and the *Ploughshares* "Literary Boroughs" blog and he has a chapter in a forthcoming non-fiction book on the films of Clint Eastwood. He lives in Reno, Nevada, with his wife Molly and their five children. This is his debut collection of stories. He can be found online at MarkMaynard.info.

ACKNOWLEDGEMENTS

There are many people who are responsible in some way for making this book happen. First, there are a few people not around to read it, yet they roam its pages. Edith Lewis and Jean, Christine and Keith Maynard, thanks for blessing me with your stories. Thanks to my mother Connie who always believed in me and taught me to love books, and my father Andy for teaching me about the work ethic required to complete anything worthwhile, and for teaching me how to tell a story. Next, my cohort members and colleagues, including the denizens of Skid Row and PGB, as well as the Purple Martins for your comments, critiques and most importantly your camaraderie. Without the careful reading and mentoring of Brad Kessler, Dodie Bellamy, Leonard Chang and Rob Roberge, these stories would never have made it out of their manila envelopes and into book form.

I would like to express my gratitude to Torrey House, especially Anne Terashima and Kirsten Allen for their diligence and care in editing the book—and to Mark Bailey for bringing *Grind* to life in its current form. Thanks to Jake and Tyler who watched their father typing away for years, and whose love of books continues to keep me reading and writing.

TORREY HOUSE PRESS
VOICES FOR THE LAND

The economy is a wholly owned subsidiary of the environment, not the other way around.
—Senator Gaylord Nelson, founder of Earth Day

Torrey House Press is an independent nonprofit publisher promoting environmental conservation through literature. We believe that culture is changed through conversation and that lively, contemporary literature is the cutting edge of social change. We strive to identify exceptional writers, nurture their work, and engage the widest possible audience; to publish diverse voices with transformative stories that illuminate important facets of our ever-changing planet; to develop literary resources for the conservation movement, educating and entertaining readers, inspiring action.

Visit **www.torreyhouse.org** for reading group discussion guides, author interviews, and more.